Tara felt her knees actually go weak.

If she'd had any sort of grip on her senses she would have pulled away, but the way Fraser moved his lips across hers, teased his tongue between them, nibbling, taunting—it was everything in a kiss she had imagined possible but never experienced until now.

Her arms reached impulsively around Fraser's neck. The movement drew her in even closer to him and the proximity could not have felt more natural. She felt his knees grip her hips, her breasts brush against his chest, sending a deep physical ache wending through to the tips of her toes and shooting back up through her like flames. Everything about the way her body was responding to him was new. Intoxicating. Absolutely not on the agenda.

She felt powerless to do the sensible thing—to push away. Her senses were overwhelmed with the incredible maleness of him. Time took on an added dimension as she took in Fraser's scent, the movement of the well-defined muscles in his neck. Sensations flew through her in heated rushes as he slid a finger along her jawline, cupped her chin in his hand and drew from her the deepest, most life-affirming kisses she'd ever experienced.

Dear Reader

THE SURGEON'S CHRISTMAS WISH isn't just about my hero's and heroine's dreams coming true (although that's a pretty big part of it!). My dreams are coming true, too! This is my first book for Mills & Boon® and I have to say I can still hardly believe it's all real. From my editor through to all of the other Medical Romance™ writers, my welcome has been top-notch. Turns out not taking down last year's Christmas lights wasn't such bad luck after all!

While writing THE SURGEON'S CHRISTMAS WISH I actually woke up earlier and earlier every morning, because I couldn't wait to get back to the computer and spend time with my heroine-on-a-mission Dr Tara Braxton. She is funny, smart, and determined not to let men get in the way of her plans to run the Deer Creek medical ski clinic. Our gorgeous-as-they-come hero, Dr Fraser MacKenzie, definitely betrays my weakness for a man with a sexy accent, and he is a blue-eyed, broad-shouldered spanner in the works for Tara's number one rule: no men.

I hope you enjoy the wintry Christmas magic of falling in love in Deer Creek as much as I did creating it. Please feel free to visit my website if you want to chat or have any questions at www.annieoneilbooks.com or find me on Twitter at @AnnieONeilBooks.

All the best—and enjoy!

Annie O'Neil

THE SURGEON'S CHRISTMAS WISH

BY
ANNIE O'NEIL

of the publisher in any form of binding or cover other than that in which it is published and without a similar condition including this condition being imposed on the subsequent purchaser.

® and TM are trademarks owned and used by the trademark owner and/or its licensee. Trademarks marked with ® are registered with the United Kingdom Patent Office and/or the Office for Harmonisation in the Internal Market and in other countries.

First published in Great Britain 2014
by Mills & Boon, an imprint of Harlequin (UK) Limited,
Large Print edition 2015
Eton House, 18-24 Paradise Road,
Richmond, Surrey, TW9 1SR

© 2014 Sheila Crighton

ISBN: 978-0-263-25473-0

Harlequin (UK) Limited's policy is to use papers that are natural, renewable and recyclable products and made from wood grown in sustainable forests. The logging and manufacturing processes conform to the legal environmental regulations of the country of origin.

Printed and bound in Great Britain
by CPI Antony Rowe, Chippenham, Wiltshire

Annie O'Neil spent most of her childhood with a leg draped over the family rocking chair and a book in her hand. Novels, baking, and writing too much teenage angst poetry ate up most of her youth. Now, quite a few years on from those fevered daydreams of being a poet, Annie splits her time between corralling her husband (and real-life Scottish hero) into helping her with their cows or scratching the backs of their rare breed pigs, and spending some very happy hours at her computer, writing. Find out more about Annie at her website: www.annieoneilbooks.com

THE SURGEON'S CHRISTMAS WISH
is Annie O'Neil's debut title
for Mills & Boon® Medical Romance™!

Dedication

This book, without any hesitation,
is dedicated to my friend Lucy, who dared me
to try my hand at writing romances with the
unerring belief that one day I would get published.
With great thanks, my friend,
this one's for you—Annie.

CHAPTER ONE

A FREE LIFT pass was definitely Tara's favorite job perk.

Just for fun, she wove her skis in and out of the morning's first tendrils of sunlight. A fresh snowfall gave an added whoosh to the fluid switchbacks she was cutting across the black diamond slope.

Sure, she was thirty-four years old, but it was all she could do not to tip back her head and scream, *Yippppeeeee!*

A year in Deer Creek had done wonders for her psyche, not to mention her emergency medical skills. She now ran her own ski injury clinic. Well, almost her own. Just a bit more scrimping and a few more paychecks to go… More importantly, she ran her own life. It was about time.

Tara felt a smile forming on her lips as she scanned the mountainside. Only the hardcore skiers were out this early. Early enough to see dawn's blush spill over the Rockies. And with just enough time to get to Marian's bakery before all of the specials were scooped up by seasonal visitors.

Hearing a couple of exhilarated whoops behind her, Tara pulled over to a small knoll on the edge of the slope. A pair of freewheeling snowboarders wearing Santa hats hurtled past, throwing a "Thanks for moving" in their wake. As they flashed down the steep terrain, she let the silent beauty of the mountain settle around her. Who needed a Christmas tree in their living room when there was an entire mountainside riddled with evergreens?

Me. That's who. She smiled, knowing full well she was as much of a sucker for the traditional trappings of the upcoming holiday as anyone. Only five more weeks!

Even so, spending it on your own was—

Stop it, she silently cautioned herself. Spending Christmas on her own in Deer Creek was exactly what she wanted. She had everything she needed in the small mountain village. A good job, a local shop with everything from pretzels to antifreeze, a Wi-Fi connection to die for and a bakery that specialized in threatening to expand her waistline.

Besides, how many doctors saw a variation of the North Pole from their office every morning? The view from up here was insane. There was nothing claustrophobic about Deer Creek. No one stealing your research or trying to shoehorn you into a career path you never wanted. Just an honest, simple life. A life absolutely, perfectly on her own.

Tara scrutinized the scarcely populated slopes. Fingers crossed, there wouldn't be too many injuries arriving at the clinic today. Not that she minded the work. Medicine was definitely her calling. It was just that every time the doors to the clinic opened, or her radio crackled to life, it meant someone else was having a very bad day.

She knelt to readjust the clips on her boots. Another five minutes or so to the clinic and—

"Heads!"

Tara flattened herself to the small knoll as a snowboarder whistled overhead. She felt her mouth go dry and her heart rate soar. Shivers shot across her shoulders and her scalp tingled in a combination of fear and adrenaline.

What a first-class idiot!

Just a few inches in the wrong direction and she would've been the one entering the clinic. Not only was the snowboarder thoughtless—he was plain dangerous.

Heart pounding, Tara bolted upright and sped after the tall figure in racing blue as he shot down the slope at lightning speed. The broad reach of his shoulders indicated he was definitely a grown man. A very athletic man from the looks of things. Long legs, trim hips, an assured strength behind his movements. There was no doubt he knew how to command the slope.

Her brow crinkled. This was hardly the time to be admiring someone's build and athletic panache.

"Stop!" Tara knew her voice didn't carry far on the slopes—but she didn't care. Good looking or not, the snowboarder could have killed her. "Stop, you—you mountainside menace!"

Tara felt heat roil in her belly. *How dare he endanger someone's life?*

The man seemed blissfully unaware of Tara's increasingly irate attempts to get his attention. As she watched him disappear around the next bend, she felt her fury double. His type was exactly the reason Deer Creek needed doctors on constant duty.

It was just the sort of thoughtless behavior her ex would've—

Stop. Stop. Not going to go there. I am not going to go there. Something positive. Just think of something positive.

The new surgeon.

Thank goodness he was starting in a few days. Tara had been running the clinic on her own throughout the summer with the ad hoc help of the local search and rescue crew. Summer saw a steady trickle of hikers, river rafters and the occasional rock climber, but it was not as busy as the ski season. Not by a long shot.

Over the summer and fall, the relative solitude of the mountain retreat suited her. Neither did she mind the twenty-four-seven nature of the job, but having another colleague to throw ideas at was always useful when it came to sports-related injuries. Plus, with freshly opened slopes and the start of the Thanksgiving vacation, five patients a day had the potential to become twenty.

Dr. Fraser MacKenzie's résumé had genuinely impressed her. He had done ski seasons all over the world, following a five-year stint as a British military surgeon in the Royal Marines. She wasn't surprised to see that after seasons in France, Italy and New Zealand he'd wanted to add the American Rockies to his list.

Tara normally didn't hire unknown seasonal staff, but the colleague she had been relying on from last year had called just two weeks earlier to say he was very sorry but he'd just accepted a tenured position at a hospital in Banff. She could hardly begrudge him such an enviable post. The chief of sports medicine in a prime resort hospital? He would've been a fool to turn it down.

Can I trust this one to last the whole season?

She'd seen other resort clinics suffer from multiple cases of doctors jumping ship early. The call of higher mountains, steeper slopes, a fresh start in a new hemisphere.

Tara frowned discerningly as she took in the majesty of the mountains around her. The Rockies were enough for her. Heck, Deer Creek was enough for her. She shook her head, knowing full well she was hardly one to cast aspersions. Just as the season-hoppers might be fleeing their pasts, she too was in her own form of escape. Deer Creek was where she had been hiding for well over a year. And being a lone wolf suited her down to a T.

Fraser pulled up to the clinic with a professional swish. He'd done higher-level Alpine training in the military, but skiing had always been something he'd enjoyed for pleasure as well. Snowboarding was a welcome adrenaline rush to add to his repertoire.

Slipping off his boots, Fraser popped his snowboard onto the clinic's purpose-built stand and jogged, sock-footed, into the wood-shingled building. He couldn't stop a smile from slipping onto his full lips. *Mountainside menace.* That was a good one.

He felt a quick stab of guilt about his near collision on the piste with the black-haired beauty— but it was his first day of work and an emergency was an emergency. Besides, wearing a white ski suit was hardly an advertisement to your presence on the slopes. Even if it looked as though someone had poured Giselle Bundschen's body into the woman's form-fitting all-in-one. He'd been lucky he'd seen the red bobble on her hat.

Fraser was relieved to note that the building's old-fashioned exterior hid an incredibly modern clinic. The Deer Creek website had shown photos of first-aid and examination rooms kitted out with everything a doctor needed up here. Well, everything but a full operating theatre and accompanying staff. Mind you, those were close enough, down at the Valley Hospital. Just a scenic trip down to the proper town on the gondola, or in an ambulance if the weather suited, and, *voilà*—everything a surgeon could dream of.

A petite redhead with a pixie cut leaned through a pair of swinging double doors, "Dr. MacKenzie? That was fast."

What was the nurse's name again? They'd only had a quick phone conversation and he'd been paying more attention to the details of the patient. Lisa? Lise? Liesel! Liesel the nurse and Tara the doctor. He'd better get those right.

Liesel's voice sounded definitively Antipodean, despite her Germanic name. Australian, he would've guessed. If looks were anything to go by, she seemed a cheery sort. They'd work well together. Cheerful and easygoing. Just the sort of relationship he liked.

Fraser's knowledge of his new boss was pretty limited, too. Taking the job had been a last-minute move, just like the decision to leave his previous post. And the one before that.

Never mind. He was good at his job. Emergency medicine was second nature to him after his time in the forces. He had no concerns in that department.

If his employers didn't think seeing the world was a good enough reason to move on after a season on their hills, then—well—it was time to move on. Hopefully, the new boss wouldn't come loaded with it's-time-to-put-down-your-roots advice.

At the very least, he was hoping to learn something new from her. A quick internet search at the airport for Dr. Tara Braxton's background showed an impressive tenure at one of America's best orthopedic research hospitals. Then—poof—nothing until he found her in the clinic here at Deer Creek. The picture-perfect mountain resort was a far cry from the lofty heights of New York City's medical elite if ever there was one.

"Dr. MacKenzie, the little boy and his mother are in Exam One." The nurse's warm Australian voice brought him back into the room.

"Yes, sorry, love. Excuse the lack of shoes. I was just—"

A fresh blast of piney mountain air flooded into the waiting room, along with a familiar-looking woman. She didn't look pleased. Miraculously, her mood didn't detract from her take-your-breath-away beauty. Tall and slender, clearly a regular on the slopes and without a speck of make-up. Enhancing that level of natural beauty wasn't necessary. Apple-red lips, glossy black hair and creamy skin with his particular favorite, a smattering of freckles across the nose. Did those eyes of hers sparkle like starlit ebony when she was in a good mood? Fraser had seen his share of beauties in his time, but this woman hit every mark. Too bad relationships were off limits for him. The impact she'd had on him in this handful of seconds was like a fully weighted sucker punch. If ever someone had presented a need to re-examine the rulebook, this woman was it. In spades.

"I am going to have to have a word with the

snow patrol. They need to start at dawn," the woman growled in Liesel's direction, oblivious of Fraser and his approving gaze. "Someone's got to crack down on these hillside hooligans!" He watched with amusement as her eyes moved from Liesel's bewildered face to himself. Here it comes, here…it…comes! The not-so-slow dawn of recognition.

"You?"

"If 'hillside hooligans' or 'mountain menaces' are to whom you are referring, then you've got me." Fraser grinned broadly. He watched as she physically recoiled from him. *That was a new one.*

He pulled himself up to his full height as she fixed him with a potent glare. *Wow.* Usually a smile won the ladies over. This one clearly had her own set of hurdles to jump. He dropped the smile and jokey tone. He was a doctor and a patients' needs came first. Posturing was a bunch of nonsense. She was going to have to get a grip and act like a grown-up.

"I am sorry for having distressed you, but I'm afraid I've got an emergency here at the clinic. So, if you'll excuse me?" He turned towards the examination room Liesel had indicated held the patient.

"What? Wait a minute!" The woman's voice hardened. "This is *my* clinic, so I think you'll find any patients waiting here will be for me. Me or a Dr. MacKenzie, who's meant to appear later in the—"

Tara felt her mouth go dry for the second time in less than five minutes.

"Wait a minute. *You're* Dr. MacKenzie."

"Nice to meet you." Fraser instinctively glanced at the exam room, hoping this interrogation would end fairly quickly. Then again, this wasn't strictly the best way to meet your new boss. "Dr. Braxton, I presume?"

Fraser offered her another smile, this time secretly enjoying the pretty flush of scarlet creeping into Tara's cheeks as he extended a hand towards her. *Good.* He did have an effect on her.

Tara curtly took his proffered hand and offered a quick one-two, business-only shake. *Was she always this spirited or was it exclusive to nearly being run over by a new colleague?* He suspected the former.

"Excuse me, doctors." Liesel's voice broke through the tension-thick air. "We've got a little boy in here with a black eye, a potential concussion, sore wrist and a very worried mother."

Tara wished she could scrub away the flush of heat from her cheeks. Unlikely, as Liesel's comment only caused it to deepen. Fraser MacKenzie had actually taken her breath away and she wasn't happy about it. Not in the slightest. Particularly as she had worked so hard to separate work and emotions. The last thing she wanted to compromise was her professional duty. And she was most certainly not going to let a gallivanting snow jockey get the upper hand.

"Of course. Sorry, Liesel. Why didn't you radio me?"

"I tried, but you didn't respond." Liesel glanced at the clipboard she held in the crook of her arm. "The little boy's mum, a Mrs. Carroll, was so anxious I rang Dr. MacKenzie on the off chance he was nearby and he said he'd race over."

"He raced over all right," Tara muttered under her breath, as she moved her hand down to her belt to check her radio. The little green light wasn't shining.

"Dead batteries?" His smile was friendly but Tara was sure she could hear a patronizing tone in Dr. MacKenzie's voice. "Could've happened to anyone."

"Batteries often freeze at high altitude, as I'm sure you know." Tara quirked an eyebrow at him and forced the corners of her lips to turn upwards into a bright smile.

Why couldn't he just keep his mouth shut? Tara felt like kicking herself—and kicking Fraser MacKenzie. Did his eyes really need to twinkle with delight when he rubbed in what a schoolgirl error she had made? This was hardly a competition for who could be the better doctor.

Batteries frequently froze up here at high elevation. Fact.

Even so, it was a stupid mistake. What if she hadn't been near the clinic and a patient required critical care? She'd have to renew the vigor of her checks every morning and stick a spare pair of batteries into the insulated pocket of her ski suit before she went out. More importantly, even if Fraser did make Braveheart look like a wimpy nerd, she needed to make sure this encounter ended with her new employee understanding who ran things here. And it certainly wasn't him. She began to unzip her ski jacket and put on her best charm-school voice.

"Dr. MacKenzie, since you haven't had a chance to settle in, I'll take this patient." Before he could protest, she slipped past him and opened the door, forcing herself to look up into those blue-as-a-lake eyes before she disappeared into the exam room.

"Are you happy to show us what you're made of later in the day?"

"Perfectly." Fraser flashed her a dazzling smile, put his hand up in a mock salute and clicked his heels together.

Tara's hand clenched the door handle, nerves jangling with—what, exactly? Embarrassment? Anger? Definitely embarrassment. *Show us what you're made of?* Sweet heavens above. It was more than clear the man was made of one part gorgeous to one part devil-may-care. She might have to rejig the ratios a bit but...

Unwilling to let him see her falter, Tara dropped her gaze to the floor. Despite herself, her ire disintegrated in an instant. Fraser's socks had little cartoon snowmen dappled all over them. It was all she could do not to burst into giggles. Not that she was going to let him know he wasn't the only one with a closet affection for the holidays.

C'mon Tara. Be fair. Give the guy a chance to explain himself.

To buy herself time, Tara allowed herself a cautious visual journey back up those long legs and well-muscled torso, landing straight on those perfectly blue eyes. It shocked her to realize she'd just ogled him. At close range. *You're a doctor, for heaven's sake! Get a grip!*

"I'll tell you what." Tara did her best to let the words trip out lightly. "Let's meet for coffee at the café next door in an hour and I'll talk you through how the clinic works." Unable to resist a bit of a barb, she turned to face her nurse, "Liesel, can you let Dr. MacKenzie know where the outdoor shop is, please? He might find it a bit chilly to work out the season in his snowmen socks."

Tara quickly entered the exam room before letting the full impact of Fraser MacKenzie's tall, dark and ridiculously handsome looks sink in. Chestnut-brown hair with the perfect amount of salt and pepper at the temples. A pair of blue eyes that seemed backlit they were so bright. And the cheekbones. Knock-your-knees-out-from-under-you cheekbones. Her personal weakness.

For heaven's sake! She felt jittery enough after their high-speed run-in on the slopes. Having to absorb the fact she'd somehow hired the living, breathing image of her fantasy man—complete with a sexy Scottish accent—was too much.

"Are you all right, Doctor?"

A young woman stood up from the exam-room chair and reached out an arm to Tara as if to steady her.

"That's my line!" Tara tried to quip, hoping to retain the smallest modicum of professionalism. Patients first. Heart doing a wild jitterbug? Not an option. Not any more.

"Now, who's this?"

"I'm Henry and this is my Mom." The blond boy sitting on Tara's exam table piped up. He seemed in good enough spirits despite the worried expression on his mother's face and the large pack of frozen vegetables he held over his eye.

"May I have a look?" She took the packet from him and placed it on the exam table.

"Wow! That's one heck of a panda eye you

have there, young man." Wincing with sympathy, she continued, "I'm glad to see your mother was smart enough to bring out the frozen peas!"

"We told him to wait until we were up to put on his ski boots, but you just couldn't hold on, could you, Henry?" Mrs. Carroll smiled lovingly at her boy, but Tara could see how concerned she was.

He did have a small cut above his eye, but it wasn't bleeding. What concerned Tara more was how gingerly he was holding his wrist.

"Henry, it's nice to meet you. I am Dr. Braxton." She gave him the most relaxed smile she could muster despite the flock or herd or whatever it was of butterflies still careering round her stomach. *Thanks a heap, Dr. MacKenzie.*

"Would you like to tell me what happened?"

"Sure!" Henry smiled up at her after getting a reassuring nod from his mother. "Mom and Dad told me not to put on my boots until we went skiing. So this morning I knew we were going skiing and no one was up yet, but I was excited, so I brought my boots upstairs to try them on outside Mom and Dad's room and they fit so I started to walk downstairs to get some juice because I was thirsty and…" Here he stopped and shot an anxious look at his mother.

"Go on, you silly little thing." His mother couldn't help laughing at her son's pell-mell style of story. "Tell the doctor what happened next."

"Well…it turns out it was harder to go down the stairs than I thought and I tripped and fell and bumped all the way to the bottom." Henry gave Tara a triumphant grin.

"Looks like you showed those stairs who was boss." Tara smiled at his bravery.

"If this isn't proof my husband should've booked a cabin instead of the townhouse, I don't know what is!" Mrs. Carroll was trying to keep her voice light, but a slight waver betrayed her anxiety.

Tara smiled reassuringly. "Believe me, accidents can happen anywhere. I'm sure this was nothing you could have foreseen. Henry, do you mind if I take a look at your wrist?"

The little boy automatically pulled his arm towards his stomach.

"It's okay, Henry. I know it must hurt." Tara reached into a drawer behind her and pulled out a child's instant cold compress. Giving the packet an experienced twist and shake, she handed it to the boy. "Why don't you hold this on your wrist for a minute?" Once he had the pack resting on his arm, Tara continued, "I'd better do a check to make sure you didn't conk your head too hard when you landed." She bent her knees so she was level with his eye line. "Can you just follow my finger?"

A few tests and a soft splint later, Tara felt satisfied that Henry had no permanent damage.

"Looks like you have a resilient son here, Mrs. Carroll, but I'm afraid his wrist is sprained. I think we can safely rule out a break as he has a full range of movement despite the swelling. Forty-eight hours of rest, elevation and cold compresses should help ease the pain."

Tara couldn't stop herself from ruffling Henry's curly blond hair. She'd always imagined she'd have a little boy. A couple of them. Not that she was too bothered if they were boys or girls. Just healthy kids, part of a happy family. Ah, well. Dreams were just that. Fanciful flights of your imagination. No room for those any more.

Clearing her throat, Tara wiggled a playful finger at Henry. "Be sure to listen to your mom, now. We'll get you back out on those slopes lickety-split." Henry grinned with relief.

Turning, Tara addressed Henry's mother, "Make sure you call me if he complains of any dizziness, nausea or starts to have any balance problems. Here's a sheet listing concussion symptoms to look out for, but I'm pretty certain you're in the clear."

"Thank you so much, Dr. Braxton. This will certainly make our Thanksgiving vacation more interesting! I hope you and your family have a great holiday."

Tara's brow cinched into a furrow, her thumb moving mechanically to the finger that had once held a diamond solitaire. She was here on her own. And that's how she liked it.

"Just me and my stethoscope, I'm afraid!" Tara shook the stethoscope in what she hoped looked like a carefree manner.

"I'm so sorry, I just assumed…" The poor woman looked mortified.

"Not to worry. An easy mistake to make."

Tara held her smile until the mother and son walked out of her exam room.

Just the mountains and me. *Just the way I like it.*

* * *

Fraser grinned as the cowbell rang out when he entered the log cabin-style café next to the clinic. He'd spent seasons in all types of ski resorts, but there was something different about Deer Creek. His staff condo didn't have the usual temporary feeling hanging about it and the resort village itself, just a small main street with a smattering of specialized shops and a fire department, was…welcoming. That was it. Welcoming. The place made him feel like he'd come home. Which was rich coming from someone who'd been born several thousand miles away and had actively avoided having a permanent address for the past four years.

He felt his smile fade. Four years. Four years that would never bring his brother back, no matter how many times he went over his options that day. He'd survived. His kid brother hadn't. It was as simple as that.

Fraser shook the thoughts away and stepped up to the counter heaving with scones, fruity muffins, oversized brownies, and to-die-for cookies. He didn't usually go in for baked goods so early, but he had just snowboarded for a good hour.

"What can I do you for?" A cheerful woman behind the counter with a thick braid running down her back smiled up at him.

"What would you recommend for a man who is about to start his first day of work?"

"Ooh! New job, eh? First impressions are very important."

Fraser winced at the memory of the first impression he'd made on Tara. Definitely not a winning one, that was for sure. Ah, well. It's not strictly as if his new colleague had skied straight off the slopes of the Deer Creek charm academy.

"You will want to have just the right breakfast if you're going to cut it up here in Deer Creek." Her eyes twinkled as she put on a mock expression of gravity and scanned his options.

"If I were you, and bear in mind I made everything you see here before you, I would start with a caffe latte and a blueberry muffin because I picked the berries myself and powered up the dough with a bit of protein powder."

"That sounds good. I will need all the strength I can get today."

"And why is that exactly?" The woman leant

forward conspiratorially. "Is the new boss a bit of an ogre?"

"Exactly! Wait, no. Hmm…" Fraser reconsidered, enjoying the playful tête-à-tête with the café owner, "More like a drill sergeant in a sexy ski suit. Nothing I can't handle. Particularly if I bribe her with a few of these treats you have here."

"So your boss is a bit of a push-over, is she?"

The sound of Tara's voice hit Fraser's nerve endings before he saw her. Great. Just great. If she was going to be this sensitive about everything that came out of his mouth it was going to be a long season.

"Morning, Tara! So this is the new doc you hired?"

"You guessed right, Marian. I'm afraid I am to blame." Tara offered a hundred-watt smile to Marian and a cool half-glance in Fraser's direction. *Is that all you've got? C'mon, Dr. Braxton. You'll have to play harder than that if you want to stick in the daggers.* This could be fun.

"Oh, I wouldn't blame you for hiring this one." The café owner gave Tara a naughty grin, not even attempting to hide her approval of Fraser's looks. *And we can chalk another point up for MacKenzie!*

Tara leant forward conspiratorially, a smile playing on her lips and her eyes trained on Fraser as she addressed her friend. "Trust me, Marian, if I'd realized I'd hired a speed freak who has problems with his superiors I would've gone straight back to the drawing board."

Fraser flinched, unable to staunch the memory of his commanding officer ordering him to return from the combat zone. *So it's time for hardball, is it?* If Tara wanted to play this game, it was fine with him. He didn't have anything to lose. Not any more.

"The ink's hardly dry on my contract..."

"I don't think we're quite at that point." Tara met his gaze, the merest hint of a question in her eyes. "Are we?" It was a statement. Not a question.

No. Perhaps not just yet. *He was the one who chose when to leave. Not the other way around.* Besides, just a couple of mini-encounters with this woman and he knew instinctively she was more substance than style. And she had buckets of style.

"Will you have the regular, dear?" Marian interjected, seemingly oblivious to the verbal sparring match being played out in front of her muffin display.

"Yes, please, Marian, and could you also add on whatever Dr. MacKenzie would like as well? We wouldn't want him thinking we are bereft of manners out here in the wilds of Deer Creek."

There was that fiery glint in Tara's eyes again. How playfully or not it shone was up in the air.

She sure was a live wire. Even so, the last thing Fraser wanted was for Tara to think he was a sexist pig. Women were paramount in his life. His mother had almost single-handedly raised him and his brother, with their father's military career consuming most of his time. And his brother's wife? Well, he had met few people who could hold a candle to the strength and determination she had shown the past few years. He closed his eyes for a moment, willing the images of his family to stay behind the door he'd had to shut four years ago. They were better off without him.

"I'm afraid I can't let you do that."

"And why is that, exactly?" Tara's dark eyes held his gaze, genuinely curious.

"Because we are professionals and while you may run the clinic, I am quite able to fend for myself."

"No one's doubting your ability to buy a blueberry muffin, Dr. MacKenzie. What I *am* doubting, is your ability to accept some Deer Creek hospitality."

Fraser was a master at keeping his cool and he was damned if he was going to blow his top over who was or wasn't going to buy a blueberry muffin. This whole palaver would be a lot easier if Tara didn't make a glaring expression and firmly crossed arms look so attractive. Fraser was no chauvinist, but he certainly was about as red-blooded a male as they came.

He took a level breath and continued, "Where I come from, manners are paramount." He saw her eyes narrow dubiously. "It is not unusual for a new employee to greet their boss with a purely professional, no-strings-attached latte and a…" he glanced at the counter as Marian brought out a huge plate of pancakes and a steaming pitcher of syrup "…very impressive plate of pancakes."

Marian leaned in before Tara could respond. "Keep this one on, honey. I think we'll like having him around the place."

Tara shot her friend an I-love-you-but-you're-not-really-helping look.

Okay. He definitely had charming and suave covered. Not so sure about the "professional" part.

Good grief. *Chill out, Tara!* Fraser seemed sincere enough. And her last comment had clearly hit a nerve. Not entirely sure which nerve, but there was definitely more going on than met the eye with this man. Anyhow, she hadn't heard the entire conversation with Marian so it wasn't entirely fair to judge. *Eat your pancakes and let it go!* Besides, staring into those startlingly azure eyes of his wasn't exactly helping her focus. Neither was the fact that he had called her a drill sergeant. Maybe she'd pushed the cool and reserved boss thing a bit too far.

This wasn't fair! She had worked hard to get herself back to the fun-loving person she had always been before New York and now she was coming across all grouchy and horrible.

"I'll throw in one of Marian's salted caramel brownies for later if that will seal the deal." Fraser tipped his head in the direction of her absolutely favorite indulgence and gave her a knowing wink.

"Now, let's not go overboard." It was difficult to keep a smile from creeping onto her lips. The man was good. No doubt about it. "A plate of pancakes will suffice to give us a clean slate." Tara knew she sounded churlish but she didn't want Fraser to think his charming smile was actually making her go weak at the knees. *Which it was.* Or that his long-lashed wink had unleashed a reel of goose-bumps up her arms. *Which it had.* But she had to ignore that now and act like his boss. *Which she was.*

Arghhhh! Why didn't she ask for photos of her applicants?

"For heaven's sake, honey." She felt Marian poking her arm playfully. "Let the man buy you a brownie. You know they're your favorite and they were freshly baked this morning!" Marian adorned her sales pitch with a musical trill as Fraser put on what she imagined was his best contrite expression.

"Thank you. I gratefully accept." Tara quickly whisked her pancakes off the counter and made her way to a window table before she made a bigger fool of herself. Any more deep and meaningful eye contact with Dr. Fraser MacKenzie would be a swan dive into a danger zone she didn't want to enter. Not in a million years.

Tara took advantage of his turned back to lean her head against the cool window for a moment before pulling her fingers through her hat-head hair. She could hear Fraser laugh quietly with Marian as he settled the bill. Even across the room that sexy voice of his put her senses on high alert. Who was she kidding? Every single thing about the man had her feeling more alive than she'd ever felt and she'd only known him for a New York second. New York. The place that had taught her how important it was to be careful— guarded. To look after number one.

Sighing, she picked up her fork and stabbed at a pancake. Maybe she was a bit uptight. But that was hardly her fault. Life had taught her to be wary and Fraser was setting off all of her alarm bells. Besides, she primly reminded herself, he had nearly had a serious collision with her this morning so she had a right to be cross with him. And another thing! Did he have to be so—so *accurate* in assessing her character when they'd known each other less than five minutes? She would have to be tough. Cool. Professional.

"One gingerbread latte for the good doctor."

Uh-oh. Was that Scottish accent of his going to get her every time?

CHAPTER TWO

"How did you know to get me a gingerbread latte?"

"I had some help." Fraser nodded towards Marian, who threw a coy beauty-queen wave in their direction.

Tara couldn't help but give him a smile of thanks as he pushed the steaming mug of cinnamon-scented coffee across the table. Poor sap didn't know he was being used. Marian had been trying to set her up with just about every male with a pulse she'd met since she'd arrived in Deer Creek just over a year ago. Heartbroken. No. Heart shut. Heart shut for good. Which was exactly why she and ol' Dr. MacKenzie here needed to get things off to a more professional start.

"How's the little boy doing?"

Tick! Top marks for starting off with a work question, Fraser.

"He'll be fine, thank goodness. His wrist was

sprained, which was the worst of it. He had a small cut on his forehead, but no concussion."

"I suppose you get your fair share of sprains up here."

Tara sat back in the worn leather chair and laughed, relieved to be back on familiar terrain: doctor talk. "Not to mention broken clavicles, arms, legs. The regular business is in ligaments. I'm sure you'll agree it's the same in every ski resort, but by the end of the season you'll be examining medial collateral and anterior cruciate ligament injuries in your sleep!"

He liked how her eyes crinkled when she laughed. In fact, Fraser liked how Tara's whole face lit up when she spoke about medicine. It clearly fuelled her.

"Oh, and I forgot to say, I do a couple of voluntary shifts every couple of weeks at the local hospital in the ER. I'm sure Valley Hospital would welcome it if you followed suit but it's by no means required."

"To see patients from the clinic?" Fraser was impressed. Tara really seemed to see things through with her patients.

"No, not really. I mean, if they're there, obviously I'd see them, but it helps me keep all of my skills up to speed and, more importantly, I don't want the locals thinking we are a bunch of elite medics who swan in and out with the good snow. It's mostly about giving a bit back to the community. Proving we're here for the long haul."

Fraser's grip tightened on his coffee mug. *Ouch.* That one had hit a bullseye.

"How about altitude sickness? Much of a problem with that?"

Tara pushed her lips forward in a let-me-think-about-it-for-a-second expression. She was clearly unaware of the fact that her thinking pout was about as close an invitation to give her lips a languorous après-ski kiss as you could get. Fraser shifted in his chair. Lasting this season bachelor-style was definitely going to be a bit tougher than he'd thought.

"Not too much," she continued, oblivious to the not-necessarily-unpleasant sensations Fraser was experiencing. "I've only been here a year or so, but the only altitude sickness case I've come across was a couple who went heli-skiing who hadn't been before. The chopper crew got to them before any of their symptoms became too severe and we were able to get them home safely."

Helicopters. Fraser felt his lips twitch involuntarily. He hadn't been behind the controls of a helicopter since… Well, long enough that he shouldn't be having a physical reaction at the mention of a helicopter. Maybe he should've talked to someone about it when he'd had the chance. Someone in the forces.

Who was he kidding? It had only been recently he'd felt anywhere near being able to speak about that day. But not to just anyone. If he were to open up, which was unlikely, he would need to speak to someone who could understand precisely how scarred he felt. The chances of finding someone else who could understand what it was like to be responsible for their own brother's death, leaving his wife a widow and two children fatherless—well—they were pretty small.

"Many deaths?" It slipped out. Sounded too keen. He felt a scowl form.

"No. Sorry to disappoint you." Tara's dark eyes turned quizzical, obviously wondering why a lack of extreme trauma would upset someone who'd taken the Hippocratic oath to care and protect.

"We do get the odd spinal injury, and the rescue crews have seen their share of fatalities over the years. To be honest, I try not to dwell on the extreme cases, because it just means someone's life has gotten a whole lot harder."

Fraser sighed heavily, nodding in agreement. He could relate to that. "It's part of the job. Seeing people's lives, their dreams, come to an abrupt halt."

Tara felt herself examining Fraser more closely. The cavalier guy who'd been trying to win her over with her favorite coffee seemed to have been spirited away. There was something he wasn't telling her. Something dark. Was he lost in the same black hole she'd been pushed into after her ex had betrayed her? She scanned his face. Maybe she'd been too quick to judge.

Don't go there, Tara. He's male. Emotions only run skin deep. No loyalty.

"Listen." She stabbed her fork into a final triangle of pancake. "I'd bet none of the injuries we have here are different from what you've seen at any other ski resort. Probably the biggest difference up here in Deer Creek are the bears."

"Bears?" Fraser felt his eyebrows raise a little too high. Had his voice risen too? Unlikely.

Tara laughed and clapped her hands, "You should see yourself! A big strong man like you getting all nervy over a little grizzly bear."

So she thought he was big and strong, eh? That was a plus. *Little grizzly bear?* Yeah, right. Fraser cleared his throat, trying to regain some professional composure.

"What do you do in the cases of a severe injury on the slopes?"

"The ski patrol up here is really good," Tara enthused. "The boys work on the same radio frequency as we do and they are all trained to a high level of first aid. In fact, a couple of them are the local ambulance medics during the summer, so they know their stuff."

Fraser felt himself nodding along with Tara's breakdown of how the ski support staff all worked together in Deer Creek. Sounded like a smooth operation. Good blueberry muffins as well. He could definitely do with one of these every morning.

As if on cue, Tara's radio began to crackle to life with the ski patrol radio tag. She pulled it off her belt and set it between the two of them on the table.

"Morning, team." They heard the male voice continue, "Afraid we've got a fifty-three-year-old male presenting with a cardiac arrest. Ski Patrol Unit One is administering CPR. They are about five minutes out from the clinic on the Starlight Slope. Tara, do you read? Switch to Channel Two. Over."

Tara simultaneously picked up the radio and rose from her chair. Speaking into the radio, she gestured for Fraser to follow her and gave Marian a quick wave goodbye. "We're on our way to the clinic now. Do you need an AED on site? Over."

"Negative. Patrol has a defibrillator on the ski-doo. Prepare for arrival of patient. Over."

Tara pulled on her jacket, giving Fraser a concerned glance. "Are you sure you're up to starting now? You're not scheduled yet."

"You bet your woolen socks I'll help." Fraser was all too aware that the first few minutes after a person suffered from cardiac arrest were critical in terms of maintaining an oxygen-rich blood flow to the body's vital organs. Compromising those precious opportunities just because he wasn't on a roster? Not a chance.

As they jogged the few yards to the clinic, Tara looked up at slopes at the sound of the approaching skidoo. The ski patrollers were highly visible in their bright red jackets with white crosses on the back. She saw one of them administering CPR whilst riding on the rescue stretcher with the patient.

Not a good sign.

Tara ran into the clinic, calling out to Liesel about the incoming patient.

"Already on it!" replied the nurse, pulling open the double doors to the trauma room housing all the necessary equipment.

Tara did a quick scrub at the sink and turned round to see Fraser carrying in the stretchered patient along with one of the patrollers. Good to see he wasn't afraid to lend a hand. On Fraser's quick count, they shifted the man to the exam table.

"How long has he been out?" His voice was all business.

"Two to three minutes max. The patient is suffering pulseless ventricular tachycardia," came the reply. It was Brian, an EMT based in the Valley. Tara had worked with him on a couple of river rescues over the summer. Reliable. He would've been doing all he could. "You guys need me in the room?"

Tara looked up quickly at Fraser, "I think Dr. MacKenzie and I have this one?" He nodded a quick assent, simultaneously unzipping the man's jacket to reveal a skin-tight ski shirt.

"Scissors?"

Tara quickly pulled a pair out from a drawer and handed them to him, while steering the heart-rate monitor to the head of the gurney.

"Update before you go, Brian?" Tara worked as she spoke, reaching for the defibrillator.

Brian spoke from the doorway, giving the doctors room around the patient, "We administered on-site CPR for three minutes and confirmed chest rises, but no pulse. We administered one shock from the defibrillator, and received a weak pulse and heart rate. We then lost the pulse after loading the patient onto the rescue stretcher so I continued to administer CPR until now."

Tara thanked Brian, who slipped out of the room as Fraser efficiently cut away the clothing surrounding the man's chest, applied lubricant and stood clear in order for her to apply the shock from the defibrillator.

They both stood completely still for a moment, waiting for the tell-tale beeps on the heart-rate monitor. Silence. Silence.

They repeated their motions—each working wordlessly—only looking to one another for confirmation of the other's movement. Eighty percent of patients could survive a heart attack with prompt defibrillation.

Tara increased the charge. "Clear!"

Fraser stepped back.

They waited again, listening, watching the patient for signs of a response.

Silence.

Beep. Beep. Beep.

Tara heaved a sigh of relief. They'd done it. She looked up at Fraser and received a broad smile of confirmation. A shot of heat poured straight into her stomach. Espresso hot and just as stimulating. *Uh-oh.* She hadn't experienced girly flutterings like this for some time. A long time. And that was just the way she liked it. Clean and simple. No feelings. Just medicine.

She tried to shrug away the growing suspicion that working with Fraser would be much more than "just medicine." They'd saved this man's life. With medicine. And now just one lovely, warm smile and her knees were going all wobbly. Terrific.

"Arthur Jones."

"What?" Tara was jolted back into the room at the sound of Fraser's voice.

"That's his name," Fraser was looking at her with an odd expression as he held up a driver's license he'd retrieved from the man's wallet. "Arthur Jones."

"Yes, right, of course." Of course. *Really proving your worth in the doctor department, aren't you, Tara?* "Mr. Jones?" Tara rested a hand gently on the man's shoulder. "Mr. Jones?"

The gray-haired gentleman's eyes fluttered open with a look of bewilderment, "Where—where...?"

"It's all right, Mr. Jones. I'm Dr. Braxton and this is Dr. MacKenzie." Tara didn't afford herself a glance in Fraser's direction. "I'm afraid you've had a heart attack. Are you here with any family?"

"Yes, all my family." Arthur's voice was weak but audible.

"Can you tell us how to get in touch with them?"

"We're staying in one of the lodge's chalets. The Pine… The—"

"It's all right, Mr. Jones." Tara laid a reassuring hand on his arm. "We'll call the lodge and find your family for you. Right now, your job is to rest and we'll get everything organized for you."

Fraser leant back against the counter, enjoying watching Tara interact with the patient. She had a soothing nature—a good bedside manner they called it in med school. He'd reluctantly inherited the moniker Smooth Operator by his medical peers, teased for the warm responses he seemed to elicit from the female patients in particular. Any smooth operations he might've pulled off in the past few years had passed him by. He wasn't one for one-night stands and dating someone for the fleeting duration of a ski season just seemed cruel when he knew he had no intention of hanging around. He was going to have to watch himself around Tara Braxton because everything about the last few hours at Deer Creek was teasing at his psyche, asking the unthinkable, *Why not stay awhile?*

One thing Fraser knew he couldn't handle was settling down. Long term just wasn't for him.

"Dr. MacKenzie, would you mind getting Liesel to call the Valley Hospital, please? We're going to need to transfer Mr. Jones for further tests."

"What about Thanksgiving?" Arthur tried pushing himself upright on the medical trolley. Gently pressing him back down to his pillow, Tara replied with a regretful smile, "I'm afraid you will definitely have to go to the hospital. I suspect they will want to keep you overnight for observation just in case you need to have an operation." Arthur closed his eyes and let out a quiet moan. "Ginny's gone to so much work! All those pies..."

"I'm afraid pie might be off the menu for a while." Tara chuckled, gesturing to Fraser to help her raise the patient's bed so he could sit a bit more upright. "We're just going to move you into a seated position, Arthur, all right?"

After helping Tara, Fraser slipped out of the room to hunt down Liesel. Once he was happy the ambulance had been organized and family members had been contacted at the lodge, he decided to take a little nosy around the facility. Of course, he wouldn't be staying in Deer Creek forever, but he may as well be familiar with his immediate surroundings for the next few months.

Behind the reception area there was a break room kitted out with the requisite coffee-maker, refrigerator, table covered with a smattering of local newspapers and a half-finished Sudoku puzzle. The refrigerator wore the usual array of amusing medical and skiing cartoons that usually found their way into any ski clinic. A strip of coupons and flyers for local attractions were held in place by a magnet advertising a local real-estate agent. The bowling alley looked fun. The art house cinema? Maybe. House buying? He put the magnet back in place over the clipping. House buying was the last thing on his agenda.

A corridor off the room led to one other examination room with X-ray facilities. He nodded approvingly. It was a good set-up. They had everything they needed to deal with the bread-and-butter cases a mountain clinic dealt with and just enough to see patients through to a fully equipped hospital for the more extreme cases.

He worked his way back to the reception area of the clinic, where he found Tara and Liesel bent over the counter, sorting out some paperwork.

"Having a look around our humble clinic?" Tara offered a tentative smile.

"Yes." He tried to put on a hokey Southern accent. "Looks like you folk know what you're doing round these parts."

Despite herself, Tara let out a peal of laughter. Hearing a hillbilly accent was one thing, but hearing a hillbilly Scottish accent was hilarious. "You'd better watch how you use that lingo of yours, mister, or you're going to find yourself lost up some holler or another, drinking hooch with the local yokels."

Fraser laughed with her, a twist of bewilderment washing across his face, "I have no idea what you're saying, but I'll be sure to try and take your advice." Pointing at the medical paperwork, he moved back to more familiar terrain. "How's Mr. Jones faring?"

"He's doing well. Ambulance will be here in ten," Liesel answered easily. Efficiently. Tara didn't know how the nurse did it but she was clearly unaffected by Fraser's lilting brogue.

And his lovely midnight-blue eyes, and his broad chest… *Stop. It. Now.*

"Once he's been picked up by the EMTs, how about you take me on a quick spin around the village so I can get my bearings?" Fraser flashed Tara one of his full-mouthed smiles, oblivious to the incredibly unprofessional thoughts swirling round her head.

"Sure, yes. That's fine. Liesel, we'll be on the radios if you're all right manning the fort for a bit. I'll be back for the afternoon shift."

"Yes, ma'am." Liesel gave her boss a comedy salute.

Tara winced at the memory of Fraser doing exactly the same thing. Was she really such a taskmaster? Her concerns weren't allayed when Liesel crinkled her brow and chewed on her lip for a moment before asking, "You're still all right covering Thanksgiving on your own tomorrow so I can have dinner with Eric's family?"

"Yes, of course! You must! Don't be silly!" *Aha!* That was it! Now she remembered why Liesel hadn't fallen under the same spell she seemed to have been smitten with. The local ski patroller had already taken Liesel's heart. Tara had promised her she would cover the clinic over the holiday as she had no plans to celebrate it herself. Thanksgiving was definitely a family holiday—something you celebrated with loved ones. Right now, Tara's family consisted of herself. She was okay with that. But having Fraser watch her exchange with Liesel was making her behave like an over-cheery spinster. Not a winning look. Not that she cared. *Oh, mercy...*

"I'll be sure to bring you some pie if I can weasel it out of Eric's mum. I'm sure she'll make loads. Your favorite is pumpkin, right?"

"Oh, don't worry about that." Tara waved off Liesel's concern. "I'll pick up something from Marian today before she closes. I'll be just fine."

"What about me?" Fraser interrupted, putting on a forlorn expression. "What's a poor Scotsman to do with himself all alone on America's biggest holiday?"

"I—I'm going to be running the clinic," Tara faltered. She hadn't been expecting Fraser to be working for a few more days. Her plan had been a simple one. Block out the fact she didn't have her own family to celebrate her second-favorite holiday with and work in the clinic. There would probably be a few of the usual bumps and bruises that came along with skiing, but hopefully the worst thing that would happen to any of the visitors to Deer Creek was a bit of indigestion. "Besides—" she tried to cover her dismay with false cheer "—there's always Christmas!"

"Not a problem, Tara." Fraser waved off her concerned expression. "I'm sure there will be some lonely ski bunny I can lure off the slopes for a bit of hot toddy and some pumpkin pie. Don't you worry about little ol' me."

Any trace of Tara's smile vanished. "Right. Well, that's everyone's Thanksgiving plans taken care of, then."

She'd been a fool to think she could trust Fraser MacKenzie to be anything other than a typical ski-season Dr. Don Juan. What an idiot to have been so weak-willed as to even entertain the tiniest bit of pleasure at his James Bond looks. Her conscience gave her a sound rap on the knuckles. No more eyeing up Fraser as if he were a delicious piece of Christmas candy! She was here to work, to save lives, to settle down. Alone. *Stick to the mission, Tara.*

Suppressing the volley of emotions she was

experiencing, Tara knew her only option was to go to her usual hiding place—her work. "Liesel, I think I'm going to man the clinic for a bit. Mr. Jones deserves a bit more attention before he's off to the hospital and I'd like to catch up on some paperwork. Would you be so kind as to acquaint Dr. MacKenzie with the wonders of Deer Creek?"

After hearing the expected "Sure thing!" in response, Tara riffled through the papers on the desk, not daring to look Fraser in the eye. *Talk about taking the express lane to getting under my skin.*

"Surely you know a joke when you hear one, Tara."

The frustration in Fraser's voice forced her to meet his gaze, his eyes snapping with something deeper than irritation. "I don't know what you expected from me—but I'm here to work. That's it. It would be nice if the work environment was a bit more 'user-friendly'."

Tara tried to smile at his comment, but knew she hadn't fooled him. "The environment was perfectly delightful before you blew in off the slopes, Dr. MacKenzie. Just bear in mind Deer

Creek is a community. This isn't a love-'em-and-leave-'em sort of town. We take care of each other here."

Uh-oh. Too much information again. Why hadn't she just let the whole thing go? Perhaps there truly was more to his suave veneer than she was giving him credit for.

"I'll be sure to remember that, Dr. Braxton. Thanks for the social etiquette tips."

Stinging from the exchange, Tara watched as the pair quietly left the clinic after a minute or so of silent coat gathering and boot lacing. Her terse tone had affected everyone's mood. Not to mention the fact she'd betrayed her golden rule: keep your game face.

She'd done everything but break down in tears in front of the man. How mortifying. No doubt the whole of Deer Creek would know how she felt by sundown. Which was what, exactly? Like a giddy princess who thought she'd just met her Prince Charming, only to discover he was a frog?

Tara rested her head on the reception counter and closed her eyes. She felt like such a fool. Not to mention a poor loser. How could she have thought, even for a moment, that a man in the exquisitely gorgeous form of Fraser MacKenzie would be anything less than a ski-season Lothario? She was usually smart enough to see through that.

All the signs had been there. Never stayed anywhere longer than a season, flirty banter with Marian, with her. And she'd fallen for it! Hook, line and sinker. At least her body had. Now her head was in a tailspin, not knowing if she was in the right or wrong. Tara scrubbed her fingernails along the counter. *What a nightmare.*

It was so frustrating to feel this vulnerable to Fraser's charms after all the hard work she'd put in at building herself back up from nothing. Finally allowing herself to become the woman she'd always known she was. Strong. Fun-loving. In charge of her own destiny.

It was a far cry from the year-long relationship with her ex. Tara had done everything he had wanted. It made her fingers curl to think of it now, but she'd been young and so bewitched by his status at the university. Her parents had both recently passed away in a horrific car accident. It had always just been just the three of them and suddenly, whoosh, she had been all alone in the world. Their deaths had fuelled her to work even harder in medical school, where her persistence and drive had won her the best grades in her course. Then suddenly the Great and Mighty Professor, renowned orthopedist and research maverick, had not only wanted Tara to be his intern but also had wanted to be with her romantically. From chief bookworm to object of affection. Tara had been completely overwhelmed. And naïve.

At his behest, she'd attended all the research conferences alongside New York's medical elite, put in ridiculous hours and stayed in the lab well into the night, week after week. A fat lot of good it had done her.

Her trust in him had been so true, so blind, she had been oblivious to the fact all her hard work had only been so that he could steal her ground-breaking research.

Being single, she didn't mind. Having had her ex take the credit for all of the advances she'd made in orthopedic surgery? That had been the deal-breaker. And the end of her ability to trust anyone fully with romantic intentions.

After working at a couple of other labs, Tara had thrown caution to the wind and taken the job here at Deer Creek. She'd entered the community cautiously at first, but had then realized, as long as she kept her wits about her, this was the perfect place to heal. To grow. To close the doors on romance and fill all the voids with her passion for medicine.

And look at her now.

All wobbly-kneed and hot under the collar after less than a full workday with Fraser MacKenzie. Great. Just great.

Tara scanned the empty clinic and huffed out a sigh as she sank into an office chair. Blocking out the fact that tomorrow was Thanksgiving wasn't the only thing on her new to-do list. She also faced a day of sitting alone in the ski clinic with little more than a mug of lukewarm coffee and a stale packet of mint cookies, figuring out a way to clean the slate with Fraser and start again. *What fun!* If time travel were an option, she'd fast-forward to spring. If she stuck to her plan she'd own the clinic outright by April, Fraser would be gone and she'd be back in control again.

Tara opened up the packet of cookies, took a tentative sniff then pushed them to the far end of the counter. This was ridiculous. She shook her head and marched herself into her office.

Snap out of it, Tara! She had worked too hard to let herself wallow in self-pity. Mr. Jones and all the other patients she had seen and would see over the season were her priority—they were where her heart lay. If Thanksgiving came in the form of a microwave turkey dinner and a couple of old cookies, then so be it. And if Fraser MacKenzie couldn't take it as much as he dished it, too bad.

"I seem to rub Dr. Braxton the wrong way." Fraser put the comment out into the crisp, wintry air, wondering if Liesel would confirm his assessment of the situation.

Liesel gave Fraser a sidelong glance and let out a good-natured laugh. "Well, I haven't worked with Tara that long. Just a few months. Let's just say I haven't seen her dander rise up quite so quickly before. You seem to have made quite an impression on her."

"Not really the impression I was hoping to make." He tried to put on a goofy grin but it felt strained. Sucking up wasn't his modus operandi.

Problem-solving was. He had signed a contract so, for better or for worse, he was going to be here for the next few months. The last thing he wanted was to spend his days squabbling with Tara. Life was too short.

"From what I do know about her, she's pretty private. She's probably a bit stressed because she only has a few months left to pay off the rest of her loan to buy the clinic from the lodge. If I were you, I'd stick to medical issues. That's what seems to keep her happy."

Quite a commitment from someone who had to be in her early thirties at most.

"Does she have family out here?" Fraser took a stab at the only thing he could think of that would get someone to unpack their suitcases and stay put.

"Not that I know of. She's never mentioned any family at all but, as I said, she keeps herself to herself."

He knew that feeling. He hadn't mentioned his family since the day after his brother's funeral. His past he kept locked firmly away, where it belonged. Out of sight. Everyone was better off that way.

Fraser turned to face Liesel, his hands firmly squaring her shoulders to his, suddenly fuelled with the need to put things right. Whether or not he stuck around was a different issue, but he was not in the business of making other people's lives a misery. Not any more. "Let's not make this a tour of Deer Creek. Let's make this a tour of Tara's Deer Creek and see what we can discover about why she loves this place so much."

Liesel crinkled her nose in confusion, "I'm not sure I follow you. I don't think Tara would be so keen if we starting poking around her—"

"No, no," Fraser enthused, "this is to help us— help me—survive the season. It'll be like a treasure hunt, only...I'm not sure what the treasure is just yet."

The nurse laughed again, infected by his energy. "I'm still not entirely sure I know what you're talking about, Dr. MacKenzie, but I'm more than happy to join in. Although the chances are pretty high that everything you're looking for is behind the doors of the clinic."

Fraser linked arms with the redhead. "I'm quite sure there's more to Dr. Tara Braxton than the clinic." He turned towards Marian's bakery on the small main street. "Come along, Liesel, I think I know the perfect place to start."

Tara gave a short wave to the EMTs as they drove off with Mr. Jones safely secured in the back of the ambulance. His pulse and heart rate were stabilized. For now. But further extensive tests were required to ensure he didn't need bypass surgery, and they were more complex than she could carry out here at the clinic. Luckily, the Valley Hospital was equipped to do most major surgeries. Denver wasn't too far along the road if something truly complicated came their way. She had seen a couple of rescues that had involved airlifting the patients to Denver but, fingers crossed, nothing so far this season.

Refocusing her energies into her work had proved to be good medicine. Patient care was something she valued and the last thing she was going to allow her new hire to do was compromise her career. It had happened once, and it most certainly wouldn't happen again.

As the morning wore on and the steady stream of patients ebbed away, Tara felt back on her game. Composed. In control. The morning's cases had been fairly easy—a fractured wrist, a severe nosebleed and an early case of stomach upset from over-indulgence. Just enough busy work for Tara to almost squeeze images of the dark-haired Scot from her mind.

Almost.

Sending Fraser out on a tour of Deer Creek, a small resort village compromising a lodge, a few ski chalets and a tiny town center was hardly going to keep him out of the clinic for long. She could feel herself return to her old habit of chewing on her lower lip. This man was not bringing out the best in her.

Technically, Fraser hadn't been contracted to start work until the following Monday. It hadn't even occurred to her to hire someone to start work over the holiday. When she'd found out at the last minute that Tom Brady was heading to Banff, instead of renewing his contract in Deer Creek, she'd made a few phone calls. Soon enough she'd felt she had covered all her bases for the holiday weekend. There were plenty of locals who helped out with search and rescue teams if required, and the team at the fire station were all trained in first aid, not to mention the ski patrollers, who were always rostered on. Bar anything truly horrible happening—she gave a quick subconscious knock on the wooden door-frame—everything would be okay.

"Anybody home?" Liesel quipped as she entered to Tara's knock.

"Just little old me!" Tara smiled at the nurse, whom she now counted as a good friend. "Sorry about earlier." She winced apologetically. "I must've woken up on the wrong side of the bed this morning."

"Mmm…could be that," Liesel mused. She leant forward and teasingly poked Tara in the arm. "Or it could be that someone has a crush on the handsome new Highland doctor."

Tara playfully slapped away Liesel's hand. At least she hoped it seemed playful.

"Do not. I don't have time for silly crushes." *How humiliating.*

"Are you saying my crush on Eric is silly?" Liesel persisted in taunting her boss.

"I would hardly call dating someone for several months and being invited to their family home for Thanksgiving as having a silly crush."

"True." Liesel dropped her backpack on the

floor behind the reception counter and flopped into the wheeled chair, lazily swinging herself from side to side.

"Where did you leave Dr. MacKenzie, anyway?" Tara wished she could've bitten back the words as soon as they'd left her mouth. She was pretty sure they betrayed a bit too much interest as to his irritatingly magnetic whereabouts. Too much interest for her own liking anyway.

Seemingly not having heard her, Liesel turned to Tara with a big grin. "This will be my first Thanksgiving, you know."

Tara smiled warmly at her pixie-haired friend. She deserved all of the happiness she received. From the sound of it, Liesel's heart had been picked up at the beginning of a number of ski seasons and soundly dropped at the last ski lift run at the first sign of spring. She was a kind, trusting woman and, from the sound of it, was reaching a point where traveling from resort to resort had lost its luster. "It's homey here, isn't it?"

"Where, the clinic?" Tara laughed. The clinic was nice, but not nearly as welcoming as one of those little craftsman houses with all-weather porches tucked away on the hillside. Too bad her finances didn't stretch far enough to include a house.

"No, silly. Deer Creek. I could really see me staying here a while." She let out a wistful sigh.

Tara slipped into the chair next to her, joining in the rhythmic swinging of chairs from side to side.

It *was* nice here. Especially when there was someone to share it all with.

CHAPTER THREE

COULD THE RECEPTION area stand up to a third run with the mop?

Tara scanned the immaculate room.

It was Thanksgiving morning and so far she had helped a whopping single visitor on a quest for a handful of cotton balls. Full marks for keeping everyone fit and healthy on the holiday, zero for keeping her mind occupied.

She felt her shoulders slump a bit as she scanned the empty room. She wondered what Liesel was doing. No. She didn't. She knew exactly what Liesel was doing. Enjoying the early phases of the holiday with Eric and his family. An involuntary sigh escaped her lips.

It wasn't the lack of patients that was sapping her good spirits. It was the absence of a certain Scottish doctor. No. That wasn't quite right.

Tara pulled on a dark curl and chewed her lower lip. It had been a long time—if ever—that someone had made such a full-force impact on her. Talk about setting your senses on fire! She stifled a yawn, knowing full well she'd kept herself up all night doing little re-runs of the previous day. Taking a little memory-lane trip along those well-defined cheekbones, stopping for a moment to enjoy the salt and pepper temples before making a quick turn towards those eyes of his. Mother Nature had come up trumps when it came to Fraser MacKenzie.

Tara shook her head and laughed. How high school was she? Then again, Tara had never really had crushes on anyone in high school. This was all brand spanking new. She shook the lingering image of Fraser's Pacific Ocean blue eyes from her head. He was all man and had her responding to him like a giddy teen.

Tara flopped down onto the over-stuffed leather sofa that had somehow found its home in the clinic waiting room and toyed with a loose cushion button. If this was what having a girly crush was like, she was going to have to quadruple her suppression skills.

He was, she reminded herself, not unique. She'd been doing perfectly well on her own for well over a year here in Deer Creek and the arrival of a new colleague—admittedly in a six-foot-plus to-die-for package complete with thick espresso-brown hair and piercing blue eyes—was hardly going to make her lose focus. Too much trust would be involved to let someone make that much of an impact. Besides, it was hardly as if she needed Fraser MacKenzie around to have a good time.

As if to prove it to herself, Tara flicked on the clinic's music system, spinning the radio dial to find something cheery. Something she could dance to. A couple of runs up and down the FM stations and she heard the opening strains of a dance-till-you-drop pop song.

Perfect! She was alone, no one was watching, it was the ideal time to have a little boogie. There was no harm in it.

Tara cranked the volume up. It was, after all, a holiday.

She began to sway her shoulders from side to side in rhythm with the music. The beat picked up. Her feet joined in. Soon she was leaping around the reception area, singing along with the radio.

See, Fraser MacKenzie? I'm not just a run-of-the-mill fuddy-duddy. I'm still footloose and fun-loving! Unable to resist a dramatic run and slide through the swinging double doors into the examination hall, Tara felt a burst of exhilaration. *Do I know how to step it up, or what?* For good measure, Tara thought she had better try out her new move again—quick slide on the tiled floor, dramatic entrance through the door into the lobby... "I'm falling, I'm falling in loooooOOOOOOOOVVVE— *Oh, no!*"

Tara felt and heard the simultaneous crunch of door on human. She fell through the swinging doors, rapidly losing her unexpected battle with gravity. The band kept on singing, oblivious to the fact she had crash-landed directly onto Fraser MacKenzie's prostrate body. It was only a matter of seconds, but the full body connection, the cradle of his hips, her breasts pressing into his taut chest, legs tangled together, ripped through her in a sensory overload. A far too close for comfort sensory overload.

Tara leapt up in a wave of mortified apologies, switched off the radio and whirled around, only to realize Fraser remained silent. She could hear deep breaths as he clutched his hands to his face, blood pouring from between his fingers.

"Oh, Fraser! I am so sorry!" She scanned the room for medical supplies in an effort to regain control. A little body contact shouldn't be jangling her nerves to this extent.

"Happy Thanksgiving," he intoned dryly.

"Wait there, I'll get some ice."

"No. No. It's all right." Fraser rolled to his side, pressing one bloodied hand to the floor. She heard him contain a small moan as he pushed himself up into a seated position.

Tara dropped to the floor beside him, gently pulling his fingers away from his face. "Let me see if I can help." She couldn't stop a panicked giggle from escaping her lips. "I'm a doctor."

"I'm glad you think this is funny."

It must have been her nerves, but now Tara really started to cackle. "I'm sorry…" She unsuccessfully choked back her laughter. "It's just that I was feeling really sorry for myself because it was Thanksgiving and I was all alone and so I thought I'd have a little dance and the last thing I expected was to find you in the waiting room."

Too much information, Tara.

Fraser looked at her through heavy-lidded eyes. "I'm glad I helped cheer you up."

"I'm so sorry." Tara gently touched his nose.

He pulled away with a poorly disguised grimace of pain. "I think you've done enough, Doctor. I'm fairly certain my own medical training could confirm a broken septum."

Tara's hands flew to her mouth. "Oh, no! I couldn't have hit you that hard!"

"I'm pretty sure you did."

Was that crankiness or humor she heard in his voice? It was hard to tell with his hands half-covering his mouth as he pinched the bridge of his swelling nose.

"C'mon." She stood up, reaching out to help him. "Let's go into the exam room and I can clean you up and get something cold on that. Hopefully, there won't be a septal hematoma and we can just ice you up for a bit."

Refusing her hand, Fraser pushed himself up from the floor. "That's pretty rare. Some ice should do it."

"Look, Dr. MacKenzie." Tara felt her frustration rising the more Fraser refused her help. Not to mention questioning her medical knowledge.

She clenched her fists as he turned his back on her and made his own way into the exam room. "I know it's rare," she called to his receding back, "but we don't want any blood getting trapped in your schnozz if we don't have to."

"Schnozz?" He turned around, an eyebrow cocked in amusement.

"Yeah, schnozz. Don't they say that where you come from?"

Fraser took in Tara's apologetic wince and attempt to form a hopeful smile as he hoisted himself up onto the exam table.

She looks very pretty when she's not trying to micromanage everything. It was nice to see her smiling.

"'Fraid not," he countered. "Beak, neb, hooter, pointy end...but not schnozz."

"Here, put these up your nostrils." Tara laughed a full throaty trill, handing him two gauze rolls covered in antiseptic cream.

"You do it," he said, wanting to see more of this less guarded Tara. He handed back the gauze, his fingers lingering just a little bit longer than necessary on hers. "I'm just the patient today."

Fraser opened his legs a bit wider in order to

allow Tara to step in more closely to him. She took a handful of disinfectant wipes from the table beside him and began to carefully dab away the blood. Even through the disaster zone that was now his nose he could tell she smelled nice. Like Christmas. In her green scrubs, she was like a cinnamon-scented Christmas fairy.

For crying out loud.

Maybe he had a concussion as well.

He looked at Tara again. Her face a picture of concentration.

Nope. It was all real. She smelled wonderful and certainly ranked up there in the beautiful-woman department. Way up there.

If he weren't so busy trying not to flinch with pain as Tara wiped away the blood, Fraser realized how incredibly easy it would be to just slip his hands onto her hips and around her waist. He wouldn't have to draw her in too much further. Only a few inches separated them. A few vital inches.

Despite having been cracked on the face with a door, Fraser hadn't been oblivious to the perfect symmetry their two bodies had created when Tara had fallen on top of him. Sure, it had been fleeting, but her body had seemed to pour perfectly into his…that sort of communion was hard to come by. Her slender hips perfectly aligning inside his, the softness of her breasts on his chest. Her lips just millimeters away from his neck as she'd drawn in a sharp breath and then pulled away… It was a feeling he was unlikely to forget. Especially now with her standing those few all-important inches away from him. If he could just focus on counting those darling little freckles dappled across that nose of hers, he might stop thinking about what was happening below his waistline.

"How does it look, Doc?"

"Well, your nose is swelling up nicely, but we seem to have stemmed the bleeding." She pulled up her shoulders apologetically. "I'm afraid you're going to have one, if not two mighty fine shiners for a couple of days. I hope there isn't anyone you were hoping to impress over the weekend."

If there were, it would only be one and she is standing right here between my legs, biting her lower lip just a little too alluringly for comfort.

"Nope. No one." His voice came out huskier than he'd expected. This was not good.

"Phew! No holiday plans ruined?"

"I didn't have any plans, don't worry."

He wondered if Tara had noticed the gingerbread latte going cold on the reception counter. Or the bag of pumpkin muffins he'd sweet-talked out of Marian last night. That was about as close to "plans" as he had come in a long time. Perhaps the busted nose was a reminder that even the slightest attempt at anything more than a professional relationship was a certified no-go area.

"What about your ski bunny?" Tara's tone was light. Or was there just the tiniest bit of crispness about it?

"What?"

"I thought you were going to seduce some rich ski bunny off the slopes and into your..." She let the sentence hang unfinished between them.

"No one said she had to be rich."

Tara turned away abruptly, busying herself with clearing up the bloody swabs and gauze littering the exam table. She snapped off the disposable gloves she'd worn to clean away the blood and let the lid of the waste-disposal bin slap down with a sharp clang.

"Tara, stop."

"Stop what?" She continued clearing up, fastidiously avoiding his gaze.

Fraser reached out, taking one of her hands in his. The heat of their connection crackled like a high-speed zip wire up Tara's arm, reverberating expressively down her spine. *None of this is very professional!*

Unable to extract herself from his grip, she felt herself being pulled towards him, back to that danger zone where she was close enough to breathe him in, to smell that all-male scent that made her a bit more light-headed than she could ever admit. Too close. Standing between his knees, face to face...the proximity was overwhelming. Fraser's eyes connected with hers. They asked so many questions. Questions she couldn't begin to answer for herself let alone for him. How was it possible someone she'd known for so little time could make the whole world around her disappear, leaving only the two of them?

She wasn't ready for this. Didn't *want* this. Lowering her eyes, she couldn't resist pausing to take in the dark stubble on his cheeks, his chin. Those lips of his, lips far too near her own. They

looked full and incredibly male. She wondered…
No. She didn't.

She hadn't even thought of kissing anyone, let
alone *wanted* to kiss anyone, in well over two
years.

Thanks for nothing, Fraser MacKenzie. That
track record was now officially over.

"Tara, listen to me." Fraser's voice was low, a
ragged murmur sending shivers through to her
very core. "There are no ski bunnies. Rich or
otherwise."

"It's none of my business. I had no right to
comment on how you lead your life."

"How I lead my life is off limits for judgment."

Her brow crinkled with confusion. Their proximity to each other screamed of intimacy yet his
words were the polar opposite. Alarm bells rang
inside her head. She steeled herself and dared to
raise her eyes to his. "What do you mean?"

"I come into a town. If I do anything other
than my work, I make a mess of things. So I do
my job. Then I leave a town. Plain and simple."

She tried to take a step back but his hands held
her firmly in place between his thighs. She was

finding it harder to breathe. "Thanks for letting me know what to expect."

He'd signed a five-month contract so she'd known from the get-go he wouldn't be around forever. Even so, she had hardly expected him to up stakes in the first forty-eight hours.

"Tara, look at me," Fraser demanded, a finger tipping her chin upwards to meet his eyes, now a storm of emotion. "What day is it?"

"Thanksgiving."

"And what is Thanksgiving about to you?"

She felt a catch in her throat. *Why was he doing this?* She thought she had steadied her voice but was immediately mortified to hear the amount of hope laced within her words. "It's about being with people you care about."

"Tara, I…" Fraser faltered, wanting to get his words right. For some reason, clearly expressing himself to her was important to him. Tara was important to him. Without a second thought he chose the only option available. He wrapped his hands firmly around her hips, pulled her in tight and began to kiss her as if his life depended on it. Perhaps it did, what did he know?

Fraser was no longer thinking. Just tasting, experiencing, enjoying kissing her. He felt encouraged as he sensed Tara's cherry-red lips respond to his. Tentatively at first, and now with the same hunger he felt. He had no idea how he was going to follow through on this, whatever "this" was. Neither did he know how he would see out the season with her. Perhaps he wouldn't. But being with her, tasting her, holding her close to him? For this exact moment it was all he wanted. She was all he wanted. How to get out of it? He'd figure it out later.

Tara felt her knees actually go weak. If she'd had any sort of grip on her senses she would've pulled away, but the way Fraser moved his lips across hers, teased his tongue between them, nibbling, taunting—it was everything in a kiss she had imagined possible but had never experienced until now. Her arms reached impulsively around Fraser's neck. The movement drew her in even closer to him and the proximity could not have felt more natural. She felt his knees grip her hips, her breasts brush against his chest, sending a deep physical ache wending through to the tips of her toes and shooting back up through her like flames. Everything about how her body was responding to him was new. Intoxicating. Absolutely not on the agenda.

She felt powerless to do the sensible thing—to push away. Her senses were overwhelmed with the incredible maleness of him. Time took on an added dimension as she took in Fraser's scent, the movement of the well-defined muscles in his neck. Sensations flew through her in heated rushes as he slid a finger along her jaw, cupped her chin in his hand and drew from her the deepest, most life-affirming kisses she'd ever experienced.

If this hadn't been the last thing in the world she should be doing, Tara would have quite happily stayed in Fraser's arms forever. As the thought flitted through her head, her stomach constricted and then froze as her emergency response radio crackled to life. She pulled away from Fraser's embrace, fingers flying to her lips, now swollen with his kisses. Her body already felt cold where his arms had held her.

Why, why, why? Why had she let this happen? Tara found herself staring into Fraser's eyes, desperate for an answer, as she tried to focus on the static-laced voice coming from her radio.

"Tara, this is Ski Patrol One calling in from the Crystal Falls Run. We've got a broken right leg coming your way. Compound fracture. Sixteen-year-old female with parents in tow. Do you read me? Over."

Tara grabbed the radio, willing herself to speak with at least an ounce of decorum. "Ski Patrol One, this is Tara, ready and waiting. Will call ambulance. Over."

"Tara, I'm—"

"Sorry, Fraser. I can't do this now." Cheeks burning she quickly crossed the room and pulled open the exam-room door. "I've got to get your blood cleaned up out of the reception area and call Valley Hospital for an ambulance before they get here. I've only got a couple of minutes."

"Right, of course. Is there anything I can do?"

"Not now. You'd best go back to your condo and put some ice on that nose of yours. You should be all right for work on Monday."

"Absolutely not. I'm staying right here." He stepped off of the exam table and in two quick strides caught her fingers with his own. She bristled at his touch. "Tara, don't be silly."

She couldn't do this. Not now. Not ever. She stood rigidly, unable to answer him.

Physically turning her to face him, Fraser gave her shoulders a quick up-and-down rub, as though he were priming someone to run onto a sports field. Not a good move.

"I'll clean up the reception area. It's my blood after all." He gave a half-smile before continuing, "You get the X-ray room ready."

"Look, Fraser. I run this clinic and what I say goes."

"Not when there's an emergency and you're understaffed."

Tara felt herself shake her head, willing the riot of sensations running through her to cease and desist. Of course what he said made sense, but why did everything he say make her feel as if she was losing control? She'd come here to regain control over her life, not to let it slip away. Just focus on the patient, Tara, not on Dr. Luscious and his delicious lips. She clenched her jaw before meeting his gaze evenly. "Clean yourself up and once I assess the patient *I* will determine if I need your help."

"Fine," he replied, beginning to gather up used cleaning supplies. "What sort of facilities do you have in place for compounds?"

"Everything we need for an immediate response. Our only big concern is if an aneurysm or infection occurs. As you know, blood clots aren't uncommon and can be lethal. If the wound gets infected, septicemia is a problem as well."

"Right. So calling an ambulance is standard?"

"It's procedure as we don't have the best overnight facilities here at the clinic, particularly for someone with a compound fracture. The patient will need twenty-four-hour nursing care for at least a couple of days, if not more." Tara slipped through the door into the X-ray room, all business now.

Fraser heard switches being flicked into position and the machines powering up. He scanned the reception room, quickly locating the mop and bucket in a broom closet. He sterilized the floor and gave himself a quick scrub up. One quick glimpse in the bathroom mirror and he could see he wasn't exactly going to be a pretty sight for a patient in pain. Come to think of it, he didn't feel so great after his run-in with the door. Funny how he hadn't felt a thing when he'd been kissing Tara. Holding her in his arms had been the most natural thing he'd experienced in years. It had been like... He barely wanted to let the thought register.

Blocking it all out would have to work right now. He grinned to himself. Denial. A man's best friend!

Tara appeared in the reception room a few moments later, fluidly pulling on a fleece over her scrubs as the buzz of the approaching skidoo became audible. Her demeanor was efficient, charged with readiness for her patient. Fraser couldn't help but admire her. She clearly lived and breathed preparation. In a world where everything that came in her clinic door was an unknown, there was little doubt she had the strength to take it on. Her tenacity for life and for medicine seemed ready made to enable her to face anything. And *anything* was what you got up here in a place like this.

It was one of the reasons he'd chosen ski clinics after the military. Every single moment of every single day was different. He loved learning, helping, changing and being challenged. The challenges of conflict zones had charged him intellectually, but living on that sort of adrenaline and coping with the high doses of the cruelty of war weren't sustainable. The closest he came to replicating the thrill of the unknown was up here in places like this. Mother Nature was boss and you had no choice but to follow her lead.

"Fraser, I really think you ought to go—"

"I'll just help you see in the patient." He cut her off, aware he was almost visibly raising her hackles. "I want to make sure you don't need a second pair of hands."

Tara glared at Fraser, furious he wouldn't just leave her alone and angry with herself for feeling relieved he was staying. Compound fractures were tricky things to reset. Immediate surgery was often required, particularly if the break at the skin had any debris in it. There had been another fresh snowfall last night, meaning the slopes were pretty clean. The patient could be lucky. But if an infection got into the bone, multiple surgeries, lengthy spells on antibiotics and long-term health problems faced the teen. At the very least they would have to soft-set the break for the ambulance trip down the mountain to the Valley Hospital, where she would most likely require surgery. Worst-case scenario—she'd need a medevac immediately.

"Here, you had better put this on." She handed Fraser a clean surgical gown from a cupboard and pointed to his blackening eyes. "You sure you're going to be all right?"

"Can't feel a thing."

At the very least Fraser knew he could pat himself on the back for his ability to pass off white lies. In reality, he could feel a myriad of sensations. Tara had set off an emotional turbulence within him he'd have to quash for the sake of the patient. *Never mind.* He pressed his lips together tightly. Repressing emotions was his personal forte.

"They're here."

Tara pushed out of the door, Fraser following her lead into the biting cold to greet the team on the skidoo. A middle-aged couple skied up behind the rescue team, faces laced with anxiety.

"This is Leanne Soames, sixteen-year-old girl

presenting with compound fracture, presumably the tibial-fibular." A red-hatted ski medic recited the stats as they unclipped the stretcher from the skidoo.

"Any possibility of hypovolemic shock?" Fraser's focus on the blood covering Leanne's sky blue ski suit was laser sharp.

"Negative. Blood loss has been minimal. We happened to be passing as the accident occurred."

On a quick count, the ski patrollers lifted the stretcher and, with the help of Tara and Fraser, carried Leanne into the clinic, her parents close behind.

Looking into the girl's terrified face, Tara smiled gently. "Leanne, I'm Dr. Braxton and this is Dr. MacKenzie. We're going to get you something for the pain straight away."

"Am I going to be okay?" Fear laced the young woman's whisper, her complexion drained of color.

"Dr. MacKenzie and I are going to do everything possible to help you heal properly." Tara realized with a start that she felt complete and utter confidence in offering Fraser's assistance as well as her own. Her declaration had come naturally.

Normally, she liked to work with a doctor for a couple of weeks before passing judgment. Fraser's ease, his confidence when treating a patient had already made an impact. Her gut told her any patient under his care had little to worry about. They could trust in him fully. She was sure of it. *If only she felt as safe.*

Tara didn't risk eye contact with Fraser, instead catching the glance of a familiar ski medic across the stretcher from her.

"Eric! I thought you were off today!"

"I am!" Eric waved away Tara's concern. "One of the guys scheduled on today had a flat tire so he's going to be a couple of hours late. I said I'd fill in until he could get up the mountain."

"Phew! I know Liesel's been looking forward to her first Thanksgiving. You'd better not let her down or you'll have me to answer to."

"Don't you worry, Dr. B. My mom's already got her busy making cranberry sauce and heaven knows what all else. She'll get a good Turkey Day all right!" He shot Tara a playful wink as the team carefully transferred Leanne to the waiting gurney. "Okay, there, Leanne?" Eric leaned over the ashen-faced girl and gave her ear a little tweak. "You've given your parents a heck of a fright. Make sure you try and get some pumpkin pie later, you hear?"

"Okay, thank you." The girl's voice was barely audible but she managed a weak smile for the curly-haired medic. It was easy to see why Liesel had been attracted to his sunny personality.

"Thanks, Eric. Any allergies?" Tara nodded in Leanne's direction.

She gave him a nod of thanks as he confirmed Leanne was allergy-free. "You go on now, we've got it from here."

"Great! I'll just get her parents settled in the waiting room."

"Thanks, Eric. You're a gem." Tara looked across the gurney, forced to connect eyes with Fraser. He was all focus now, fine-tuned to the task at hand. *Good.* After a quick nod from Tara he began, "Leanne, we are going to give you a local anesthetic for the pain. Have you ever had one before?"

"No, never."

Tara gave her a reassuring smile. "It's all right. You'll be awake, you just won't feel the pain as we reset your leg."

Tara and Fraser set about prepping Leanne for X-rays. She was given a strong enough dose of painkiller to take away the immediate pain but not enough to fully sedate her. She was quickly put on an antibiotic drip and, after finding out she hadn't had a tetanus shot in over five years, Tara injected the correct dosage and assured herself that the teenager's vital stats would enable them to take her to X-Ray.

Next, Fraser helped Tara to cut away the girl's ski pants. They cleaned the wound as best they could, and set Leanne's leg in position for X-rays.

As they worked, Tara was struck by a sense of *déjà vu*. Working with Fraser was as organic a thing as she had ever experienced. They shared a quiet efficiency of movement and speech as they worked, each gently informing and assuring Leanne with every step they took. She admired the care Fraser took to ensure not to alarm the teen as it became clear she would require surgery on at least two torn ligaments as well as likely require screws in her broken bone, such was the severity of the break. It was a surgery they wouldn't be able to perform here at the clinic because of the limited facilities.

"Do you mind calling Valley Hospital for me, Dr. MacKenzie? We need to book an ambulance and OR for Leanne as soon as possible."

"Sure thing, Dr. B."

Fraser had turned to make the call before Tara could catch his eye, but she was sure she had heard a healthy dose of humor in his stolen nickname for her. *Original?* No. *Sending a nice lazy swirl of heat through her stomach?* Definitely.

"Leanne? I'm just going to check your X-rays in the next room, all right?"

After receiving a murmured assent, Tara pushed through the swinging door into the central corridor of the treatment center. As she pushed the X-rays up against the lightbox she was suddenly very aware of a six-foot-something presence behind her—one she was pretty darned sure had a Scottish accent.

"Compound fracture to the tibial-fibular, as predicted. Your ski patrol boys know their stuff."

Tara felt a blush of pleasure spread across her cheeks despite the fact she knew she didn't have a single thing to do with hiring the ski patrollers.

"Nothing to do with me," she quipped, hoping he couldn't see her flushing like a schoolgirl.

"Well, I know something that has a lot to do with you…" Fraser drew out his sentence as if daring her to guess what he was alluding to.

Tara turned around so quickly she hadn't realized how close Fraser was standing behind her. Her hands flew to his chest to steady herself and just as quickly she withdrew them. Touching Fraser anywhere, let alone on his muscular chest, was beginning to severely curtail her verbal skills.

"Don't worry, Tara. I don't bite."

"Of course not. Don't be silly, I… You just startled me by being right…there." *Winning comeback, Tara.*

He looked down at her with a quirked eyebrow. "Shall we get to Leanne and start the re-alignment?"

"Absolutely. After you, Dr. MacKenzie." And another conversational gold star! Being mute might be an option for the rest of the season.

Back in the exam room, Tara felt her senses realign themselves. This was her element. Her zone of focus. With Fraser helping to limit movement from Leanne, Tara deftly re-aligned the broken bones in order to prevent the fragments from causing further soft-tissue damage. Together, they applied sterile dressings to the open wounds then encased her leg in a soft-set splint that she would wear until she was ready for surgery. Fleeting thoughts of her research, which focused on exactly this type of injury, flew through her head. If she owned the clinic and could save some more, perhaps the research could go ahead one day... She shook the thoughts away. Not possible. Her ex "owned" the rights. Only a hospital could afford to buy them. Owning the clinic was within her reach. Buying back the intellectual rights to the operating technique—*her* operating technique? Way out of her price range.

Tara relinquished her spot in the ambulance so Leanne's parents could ride along with her. There were two EMTs on board, so any concerns that might pop up in the hour-long journey to Valley Hospital could be dealt with.

Leanne's parents, whilst clearly worried for their daughter, were able to make some half-hearted jokes about raiding the closed bakery so they could sneak some pie into the hospital they would undoubtedly be spending the next few nights in.

After waving the ambulance off, Tara gratefully re-entered the warm clinic. Pulling her hair out of the ponytail she'd bundled it into when Leanne had arrived, Tara allowed herself a moment to close her eyes, lean against the clinic wall and take a few slow breaths. She sure could do with one of Marian's lattes right about now.

"A lukewarm gingerbread latte for your thoughts?"

Her eyes popped open at the sound of Fraser's voice. A voice that caused one too many thoughts she sure wasn't ready to share with him.

"It's after lunch. Marian's closed for the holiday at noon, I think." *Wow.* And strike three in top comebacks of the year award!

"Not unless you plan ahead!" Fraser's eyes shone merrily as he pulled a tall latte cup out from behind his back, along with a familiar-looking bakery bag. He crooked a free index finger, beckoning her to come to the reception desk. "I got these earlier, but was, um, waylaid by a certain dancing doctor."

Tara cringed at the memory of their swinging-door collision. "If you don't mind it being heated up in the microwave, it would be my pleasure to zap it for you."

"You didn't have to do that." Tara felt her heart give a giddy skippity-hop. She hadn't given a single thought as to why he'd appeared at the clinic this morning. Fraser's gesture genuinely touched her. She knew it might seem small to some people, certainly to her ex who didn't "do gestures". He'd made her feel a fool more than once when she had left little notes in his pocket, a chocolate kiss in his briefcase. She'd never once received a surprise gift or otherwise from him.

Not that it was presents she was after. Sighting a spring daffodil gave her more joy than expensive displays of affection. It was the gesture that was important. Despite her ex's attempts to wean her off her "silly affectations", quiet little niceties remained her favorite way of showing people she cared for them.

But now, here, Fraser was virtually able to read her mind— *You'd better stop that thought process right now.*

"Yes." Fraser twisted the cup round with his long fingers before putting it on the counter, seemingly oblivious to the coil of heat he'd ignited in her chest. "I did. I needed to come back."

Tara looked up at him, struck by the sobriety of his voice. A shot of guilt made her catch her breath at the sight of his blackening eyes. "Whatever for?"

"I didn't think we got off to the best start yesterday."

"And today wasn't much of an improvement." Tara's hands flew to her mouth as the words slipped out.

Fraser threw back his head and howled with laughter. Hardly the reaction she'd expected. Hadn't he felt the same body-jarring wonder when they'd kissed? A kiss she would no doubt relive again and again in her bachelorette apartment upstairs once he'd gone. A kiss she could never again experience in real life if she were to keep on track as a lone wolf.

"Oh, Fraser, I—"

"It's all right," he interrupted, coughing away the rest of his laughter. "I know this can't be anything. *We* can't be anything." He raked a hand through his dark hair, clearly uncomfortable with the conversation. "I suspect you've figured this out already, but I am the last person on earth you would want to get involved with."

"Of course. Why would I want to do something like that?" Tara felt her breath constricting in her throat as she added on a fervent nod of confirmation that getting together with Fraser MacKenzie was the last thing on her mind.

He was right. Who were they kidding? She'd been doing really well on her own. Her emotional Geiger counter was barely able to take on board the heady highs and lows she'd experienced over the last twenty-four hours. Who knew what a week, a month, a lifetime of emotional tailspin with Fraser MacKenzie would do to her?

"Friends?" He held out a hand. The same hand that had tenderly pulled her close in to his muscled chest just a couple of hours earlier.

"Of course. Colleagues and friends," she replied brightly. Perhaps a bit too brightly but, of course, it was the right decision. The only path they could take. "Don't be ridiculous."

She waved away his hand, unable to trust herself to touch him again. "Go on, get out of here. You were a great help today, but you really should get something cold on that nose of yours."

* * *

As the wintry air bit at his face, Fraser felt his nose throb. Good. He deserved to feel a good wallop of pain. Pain he definitely deserved. What had he been thinking? Kissing Tara as though he was going to offer her love and protection chased up by a weak-handed offering of friendship? He would've refused to shake his hand as well.

If his brother were alive, he would have frog-marched him right back into the clinic, demanding Fraser apologize immediately. Fraser scrubbed his fingers through his hair and took a deep breath of the freezing mountain air.

It was at times like this he really missed Matt. Like a piece of him was missing. The man had had more moral fiber in him than the whole of the army. And there wasn't a damn thing he could do to bring him back.

Fraser broke a personal rule and allowed himself a few minutes to relive the worst day of his life as he strode along the snowy path to his condo. He may as well have been running a high-def video in his head. Still as crystal clear as the day it had happened. He stopped to throw a snowball at a tree to see if that helped dull the memories. *Nope. No good.*

Wiping the remains of the snowball from his gloves, he looked up to see the impressive central lodge house rising up above him at the end of Main Street. The large wooden hotel looked as though it could have been made out of gingerbread it was so picture perfect. Dusk was hinting at setting in, the slopes emptying as skiers sought out food, warmth, companionship. Through the windows Fraser could see the lodge's restaurant was alive with the happy laughter and chatter of families, loved ones coming together to share their Thanksgiving meal.

Standing still in the snow, letting his eyes flit from table to table of smiling faces, Fraser felt himself soften a little.

His behavior had been lacking. Sorely so. Taking in a deep draft of air, he let his shoulders drop as he exhaled.

Would there ever be a right time? A time to let go of the past? Somewhere in him he knew he could not use his brother's death as an excuse to keep the people he held dear to him at bay forever. He was grateful his parents hadn't been alive to bury their youngest son, but that didn't make things better. Not by a long shot. He'd left his sister-in-law and niece and nephew to deal with the numbing grief of loss all on their own. The number of times he'd nearly jumped on a plane…

Fraser changed his course and headed towards the ski lifts. Maybe a run on a black diamond would help shut down a thought process he wasn't ready to have. Yes. It had been awful. Yes. There were decisions he could have made that day that might have saved Matt. Then again, he could just as easily have become a victim of the crossfire as well. Then neither he nor his brother would be alive. And, more importantly, no one would be in a position to provide for Matt's family, as he was now. He knew the anonymous monthly deposits he made into a trust set up in their name would never replace his brother's presence, but it was something. Not that he had seen or spoken to them since the funeral. They were good people. They didn't deserve a regular reminder of their husband and father's killer.

CHAPTER FOUR

TARA'S FINGERS PLAYED idly with the aspirin bottle. She had a cracking headache and was pretty sure she knew why. A perfectly formed, six-foot-two, dark-chocolate-locked headache. Had she mentioned the crystal-clear blue eyes that made her swoon like a damsel in distress whenever she saw them? No? Well, those gave her a headache, too.

Not even three hours of patients after Leanne left, her fail-safe plan for keeping dark thoughts at bay, had proved a tonic to the pain. Neither had the missed call from New York City she'd seen on her mobile. Typical of her ex—not even enough time to leave her a message. It was how he'd always done it. She was just supposed to know that when his number flashed on her screen she was meant to be available. She was glad she'd missed the call. She hardly needed more reminders that her life wasn't strictly going as planned.

What was it about her that made men want to run away? Her ex hadn't even been able to stay faithful before fleeing the coop. Admittedly, he'd had double the reason to run, having also stolen a year's worth of her breakthrough research. Research that could have launched her career amongst the medical elite. Instead, he had taken credit for her advances in orthopedic care and had published everything under his own name. The move stamped his name on the technique and with the addition of registered intellectual rights, made him the only one who could approve other doctors performing the surgery. Classy.

She placed her fingers on her temples in a vain attempt to rub away the throbbing pain. At least the patients would benefit from her innovations one day. Which was the entire point of it all.

To be honest, the world of lab research had never been for her. She had enjoyed discovering new ways to advance patient healing, and would definitely agree to continue her research if it involved being in a hospital or clinic because being here in Deer Creek, meeting patients and giving hands-on help was exactly what she loved. She was giving frontline help to patients.

The satisfaction she felt from every single day at the clinic was a tenfold improvement on attending yet another fundraising cocktail party her ex had bullied her into attending to climb yet another rung on the social ladder. The truth was she had done the research because she'd wanted to make a difference. A real impact. And that was exactly what she had been doing here in this little mountain hamlet. Making a difference.

Now all that remained was to see if she could clean up the disastrous oil spill of emotions Fraser had unleashed in her. He was right. Friends was the best way to go. The only way to go. It was obvious to Tara she wasn't over the hurt she'd suffered in New York. At the very least she knew she wasn't ready to trust anyone romantically yet. Not by a long shot.

Fraser's arrival was serving as a potent reminder that sticking to the lone-wolf survival plan was the only way forward.

Tara flicked the aspirin bottle across the desk in a satisfying series of spins. Woohoo! This was shaping up to be pretty much the worst Thanksgiving ever.

Sighing, she looked at the big clock hanging above her desk.

Five o'clock. The lifts closed around now and she could safely shut up the clinic. Night skiing didn't begin until much later in the season and the sun had all but disappeared for the day. Most people in Deer Creek, heck, across the country, would be sitting down to plates laden with turkey, sweet potatoes and gravy about now. Just thinking about it made her mouth water. And pumpkin pie! No. Pecan. No. Pumpkin.

Both.

Her stomach grumbled. Where had she put that muffin?

Tara pushed herself up from her desk chair, fairly certain she'd left the bakery bag on the reception desk. After Fraser had left, a steady flow of patients had kept her away from the baked goods and, to be honest, she'd felt too overwhelmed by their—um—face-to-face encounter to eat. Suddenly she was ravenous.

Without looking, she knew there was only a scrap of old cheese and a none-too-inviting banana sitting in her refrigerator. If she was lucky there might be a spoonful or two of luxury ice cream lurking in the freezer behind the ice-cube trays. The hotel would be booked out. Not that she fancied sitting on her own in the midst of dozens of happy families celebrating Thanksgiving together. She sifted through the fliers spread out on the low table in the reception area by the sofa. Surely there had to be something last minute.

A red flyer poked through the array of papers. Tara pinched it between her fingers and held it up for inspection. *What have we here?*

"Turkey Burgers and Beer at Bobby's Tavern"

Great—sounded perfect. If she couldn't have roast turkey and all the trimmings, a big juicy burger at Bobby's, along with one of her unread medical journals, would be the perfect anecdote to the Thanksgiving blues.

"That'll just be a few minutes, Tara, all right?" The chef and proprietor of Bobby's offered her a toothy grin and nodded in the direction of the quieter lounge. "I know where to find you."

"Thanks, Bobby. You know me too well!" She took the icy glass of locally brewed ale from the counter, gathered her armful of magazines and headed away from the television that was blaring football scores across the sparsely populated bar. A smile played across her lips. Bobby knew the real Tara. The relaxed, fun-loving doctor who adored life up here in Deer Creek. Not the mood-swinging woman who was reacting to all of the button-pushing done by her latest hire.

Tara flopped down into one of the long sofas facing the massive stone fireplace. Who was she kidding? The Tara Bobby knew was a "new" Tara as well. More cautious. Less trusting. A lone she-wolf forging a new life for herself up here in the mountains. And up until about forty-eight hours ago…it had been absolutely perfect.

She set her beer down on the thick wooden table and grabbed a couple of cheesy-looking elk cushions. She punched some air back into them before settling back into the sofa with her magazine. *Now that's more like it.*

The side lounge of Bobby's was the perfect anecdote to a day that had frazzled just about every one of Tara's nerves. Worn leather sofas, mashed-up cushions with mountainscapes or amusing depictions of elk or bears stuffed in the corners and, of course, a merrily burning fire.

She slipped her boots off and tucked her woolen-socked feet beneath her. A few flicks through her medical journal and she would be back in a good place. Tara let her eyes run down the table of contents to cherry-pick the medical innovations and news she would read about for a Thanksgiving treat. A familiar name caused her to catch her breath and sit upright.

It was her ex. *What was he doing in the journal?* Taking more credit for her medical advancements, no doubt. Heart racing, Tara swept through the pages until she reached the article that had mentioned his name: "New Orthopedic Technique at Standstill."

Her eyes tore through the article and it wasn't until she exhaled at the final sentence that she realized she'd been holding her breath.

So. Her ex was getting his comeuppance. Not that she'd wanted revenge. Just honesty. Looks like he hadn't even been truthful enough with the medical community to admit he didn't know how to utilize the innovative research he had presented as his own. Either that or he couldn't find another researcher as naively trusting as she had been. Now his funding was being pulled and his so-called "intellectual property" was up for grabs. Not so smart after all, were we Professor?

She read the article again and felt her medical brain begin to kick into action. She could see where he'd gone wrong, why his approach to her surgical technique hadn't moved forward. Her fingers twitched, involuntarily longing to get back to work on her project. If only there was a hospital nearby that would let her begin to put what she'd researched in the lab into practice, she was sure she could make advances. Positive she could make it a worthwhile investment.

"Your burger, madam?"

Tara's senses, already on high alert, were well aware Bobby hadn't suddenly acquired a Scottish accent. A Scottish accent that sent a torrent of sensation waterfalling down her spine.

"I didn't realize you'd found yourself a new job."

"I wasn't under the impression I needed one," Fraser shot back, before putting on a comically frightened face as he set down a basket overflowing with French fries and a mammoth turkey burger. *Uuuurgh!* Why did he have to show up now? Just when she could've done with some alone time rather than being made to feel like an ogre! Or was life telling her something else? Was it time to let someone in?

Tara drew a hand across her forehead and felt her top teeth pull at her lower lip. "I'm sorry, Fraser. I just—I've just had a bit of bad news."

"May I?" His voice was quiet as he gestured at the seat across from her. Only then did she notice he was carrying a second burger basket and a precariously balanced pint of local ale.

Here goes nothing!

"You're welcome but I can't guarantee I'll be the best company tonight."

"Better some company than no company."

She watched as he settled himself into the overstuffed armchair after sliding his burger onto the table between them. He looked across at her with a level of sincere concern that was almost too much to bear. She really needed a friend right now. Could she trust him with this? He was, at the very least, a medical professional and would understand her plight. This situation wasn't just professional, though. It was about her ex. It was about her failure to know she was being used.

Not wanting to risk being distracted by those

ridiculously blue eyes just yet, she looked down into the appetizing basket in front of her and tugged out a couple of French fries.

"Would you like to tell the doctor about it?"

Fraser's voice was teasing but Tara could hear the genuine kindness behind it. How could she confide in the man who had torn up her no-contact-with-men rulebook and thrown it to the winds? Wasn't this history repeating itself?

No. It was work. Her work. Well…and some feelings. All she had to do now was trust in Fraser. Professionally. Carpe diem!

"All right. You seem like a man who likes a challenge." She leveled her gaze with his. "What do you know about distraction osteogenesis?"

Fraser listened intently as Tara poured out her story. The lauded research post, the mind-numbing hours of work leading to the theft of her innovations and the collapse of what she had thought was to be a lifelong partnership—both professional and personal. It explained a lot and he felt for her. When she had been vulnerable, she had trusted in someone to the point that he had effectively taken control of her life. From the looks of things, Tara was working as hard as possible to make sure that never happened again. Fraser scrubbed at his chin as her words hit home. *Hell.* He could give her training lessons. He could teach a Ph.D course in how to avoid getting involved ever again.

He watched as Tara distractedly pulled another French fry through the puddle of ketchup she had made in the corner of her basket. Those slender fingers had been caressing his neck not more than a few hours earlier. He tipped his head from side to side, trying to shake away the memory. Too good. Too close. Too dangerous.

As if awoken from her thoughts by his movement, Tara looked up at him with a rueful grin and grabbed her burger. "So, that, my friend, is the story of my life." She took an enormous bite of the turkey burger and through the meat, tomatoes, onions and poppy-seed bun managed to get out the words, "Happy Thanksgiving!"

He chuckled and grabbed his own burger. The girl had fire, there was no doubt about it. And what had happened to her was wrong. Plain and simple. Her ideas were groundbreaking. Impressive. She deserved to get credit for her work. Not have them caught up in the world of funding and intellectual property.

"Have you spoken to anyone else about this?" He put his burger down and took a swig of beer, his mind on overdrive.

"No. Not really. Well, no. You're the first." Tara lifted her eyes to his. Fraser felt himself shifting in his seat as he watched her top two teeth take hold of her lower lip for a little tug. This whole "friends" gig was definitely going to be a challenge.

"I don't know if I would have shown as much restraint if I had been in your shoes."

"Saying something would've felt like crying wolf. After all, I had been working in his lab with his funding and everyone knew I was his girlfriend. I'm pretty sure that's all they saw— the girlfriend part."

"Oh, I'm sure they saw a lot more than that." Fraser pulled the pickles out of his burger to avoid another chocolate-river journey into those dark eyes of hers. Her ex was a fool. If he found himself worthy of winning someone like Tara's love, the last thing on his mind would be undermining her. She was an intelligent and talented doctor as well as a knockout beauty. Whoever didn't see that right off the bat wasn't really worth wasting brain cells on. He felt a growing swell of indignation that she had been wronged. Not to mention frustration that her research was at a standstill.

"It doesn't really matter now. Two years have passed and it looks like I'm enjoying a bit of kismet."

Her comment was flippant but Fraser could see there was more to it. "But when I came in you said you'd bad news."

"The bad news is that the research has come to a standstill because the silly dolt couldn't figure out how to progress beyond the point I had reached and he's going to lose his funding if he can't make it commercially viable." She collapsed her head into hands and gave it a sound shake. "I was foolish not to cover my bases. Protect myself." Looking back up at Fraser, her cheeks were flushed and her eyes sparked with passion. "Don't you see? If I hadn't been so gullible as to believe he loved me for me and not just for how I could improve his career, all those people who are in genuine need of this technique would be getting it right now!"

"You mean you'd never go back into that world again?"

"No."

There was no questioning that response. Tara's lips were tight and her entire body poised itself defiantly, as if daring Fraser to challenge her. Then, in an instant, she softened and leant back into the sofa, folding her long legs beneath her.

"No, that's not right either. I love the research, but I also love my life here, having hands-on impact for the patients." *And hiding away from the rest of the world.*

"I thought you said you had a good relationship with the hospital down in the Valley. Wouldn't it be worth enquiring whether you could start again? See if they could plump for the intellectual rights?"

"No. I don't do schmoozing."

"Oh, I see." Fraser leant back in his chair and appraised her with an irritating know-it-all look. "So you're perfectly happy for your ex to fall flat on his face—but equally happy to let all of the patients who could benefit from your technique suffer."

"Not at all!" How could someone be so maddening and so *right* all at the same time? "It's just that I…" Tara felt herself wavering now. Of course what Fraser was saying made sense. Not continuing with her research wasn't just hurting her, it was hurting patients. She had invested so much of herself and letting it all fall by the wayside seemed foolish. On top of that, the work absorbed her. Fuelled her.

"It's just that you…" Fraser nodded encouragingly. The man may be completely gorgeous, but he was also one heck of a listener. What was it? What was the truth behind her reticence to do her research again?

I'm scared.

"I guess I hadn't thought of being able to do it on my own."

"You wouldn't be, you silly goose!"

Fraser slapped the arm of his chair and took a big gulp of his ale. He seemed to really be enjoying her plight. Or was he problem-solving? Perhaps it was the marine in him coming out. If so, the military had lost quite an asset when he'd taken to the slopes.

"You won't have your fancy New York security blanket of the establishment behind you, but who cares?"

Tara took a look on either side of her and raised her hand. "Me—it's me who cares."

"Well, of course you do," Fraser continued, a huge smile on his face. "It's your project, but can't you see you're in the perfect position to carry on your research exactly where you are? Think of yourself as David and the New York set as Goliath."

"I don't follow." *Not by a long shot, but the Fraser you are right now, he's much more my style.*

"Here..." Fraser held his arms open wide. "Carry on with your work here in Deer Creek. It's perfect. You've got exactly the type of patients needed for treatment. You've got doctors coming in and out of the clinic who would have great insight into your project—maybe even help you if you're in a tight spot, add new perspectives. It's a great theory you've been working on, Tara. All you've got to do is put it into practice."

"Easier said than done, Dr. MacKenzie," Tara parried, feeling simultaneously wary and fuelled by Fraser's enthusiasm. She was enjoying the spirited exchange of ideas. As if by some sort of magic, Fraser seemed to have made possible what she had deemed impossible. Then again, these things were difficult. They took time. And a lot of money. "Where do you propose I look for funding? All my money has been going into buying out the rest of the practice from Deer Creek Lodge. That puts the kybosh on anything else."

"Risky. Why are you putting all your eggs in one basket?"

Tara bridled. He was playing devil's advocate far too well. Just three seconds ago he had been setting up a research lab here and now the idea of staying on at Deer Creek seemed to repel him. "Because I love it here! Running the clinic makes me happy."

"Does it, now? Does hiding here in your perfect little mountain resort away from all the big bad medical professionals of New York City truly make you happy?" Fraser pushed himself forward in his seat, locking Tara into a fiery blue gaze.

"A lot happier than flitting about the globe, avoiding whatever it is you're blocking out makes you!"

The fire burning in Fraser's eyes dulled in an instant as he raised his glass in a toast.

"Touché, Dr. Braxton."

"Oh, Fraser. I'm so sorry." On impulse, Tara reached across the table and took hold of his free hand. "It's none of my business why you do what you do."

His silence increased Tara's concern that she had gone too far. He was right. How he chose to live his life was none of her business. Just as she was crystal clear that being on her own was precisely what she wanted. As if in defiance of her private thoughts, Tara felt a shot of heat run up her arm as Fraser's thumb brushed over the top of the hand that she had so impulsively reached out to him.

She forced herself to chance a glance into those deep blue eyes of his, trying her best to ignore the intense sensations hot-rodding throughout her body as he continued to run his thumb contemplatively across the back of her hand. Focus on the friendship, Tara. You need a friend right now. Nothing more.

"I suggest, Dr. MacKenzie, that we refresh our

glasses and raise them in a Thanksgiving toast to the future. Regardless of what that may be."

Fraser increased the pressure on her hand and in a swift move brought it to his lips, where he impressed a kiss upon it. A kiss that caused far too many sensations to flutter their way up, around and throughout Tara's midsection.

"Only if it includes a race down the Stag's Leap Black Diamond Run at sunrise." His eyes twinkled mischievously.

Tara turned her hand round in his to give him a solid handshake.

"You're on."

CHAPTER FIVE

"Have you ever had home-made cranberry sauce with merlot wine?" Liesel didn't even try to disguise the dreamy expression enveloping her face.

"I have," she continued, without bothering to wait for a reply.

From the nano-second the two women had opened up the clinic on Friday, Liesel had spent each spare moment between patients recounting every minute detail of what, by all accounts, had been a once-in-a-lifetime meal with Eric and his family.

Thankfully, a hot shower, a side trip to Marian's and one very large latte had put Tara in a good enough place to take on her smitten friend's blow-by-blow account of meeting Eric's siblings, his grandparents, his parents, their dog, a kiss under the newly hung mistletoe and the fact each of the aforementioned were all so *fa-a-a-a-bulous* they had all teased Eric about asking Liesel to marry him right there at the dinner table.

"Just promise me that whatever happens, you won't leave me needing a new nurse!" Giving her friend a big hug, Tara couldn't help but try and squeeze away just the tiniest bit of envy she felt at her friend's ease with being so publicly and happily in love.

Fraser had been a no-show on the slopes that morning. "Just friends" or not, it had hurt to be stood up. Tara hadn't realized how much she'd been looking forward to their ski date.

No. *Not a date.* Just a fun run down the slopes with a friend.

It hadn't helped that when she'd arrived at the clinic she'd found a note pinned to the door, apologizing for the missed race but saying that he had got up before the sun and thought he'd better go down and explore the valley. Heavy snowfall was expected to move in over the course of the week and Tara knew Fraser was wise to get his bearings now, while he had a chance. It was logical, but it didn't stop the sting of what felt a little too close to rejection.

Feeling herself being pushed out of the hug

to be examined, Tara squirmed as Liesel scrutinized her.

"He's got you bad, doesn't he?"

Bristling just the smallest bit, Tara replied tartly, "I haven't the slightest idea what you're talking about."

Liesel looked over her tiny wire-rimmed glasses at Tara, an eyebrow cocked, clearly dubious of Tara's pronouncement.

"Uhh, yeah. I'll believe that when the Abominable Snowman walks in the front door, asking for an icepack."

The two women looked at each other for a moment in taut silence then laughed.

"We-e-ll…." Tara was forced to concede, "he's all right. But if I were ever to date again, and that is a particularly big *if*, it would be with a man who would be worth the risk. Not some high-speed globetrotter."

"Earth to Tara. The man's a highly skilled trauma surgeon! I don't care what you say, but that's hot."

"True, but that doesn't mean he's good at…" Tara struggled trying to think of something on this earth Fraser wouldn't be good at. Hanging around long enough to fall in love? "I bet you he isn't any good at playing Sudoku."

"Not really a deal-breaker in my book," Liesel retorted, whirling round in her chair, her lap filled with the patient charts they'd worked up that morning.

Deciding the conversation very clearly needed to be over, Tara turned to walk into the stock cupboard, only to hear Liesel calling after her, "Particularly if dating a man who looks like he could chop firewood and talk surgery all day is your thing."

"Maybe it is!" Tara retorted, enjoying their banter.

"Maybe what is?"

The sound of her ex's voice made Tara's blood run cold. What on earth was he doing here? Maybe she should've picked up the missed call. She could have saved him the journey.

"Hello, Tara," he drawled, clearly enjoying the shocked expression on her face. "How's Santa's playland?"

"It's great," Tara replied through gritted teeth. How could she have forgotten his panache for belittling everything she enjoyed? Belittling a place that had grown so very dear to her heart.

"Why are you here, Anson?" She glared at him, heart racing, willing this entire scenario to not really be happening.

"Oh, I just thought I'd make a little visit to your winter wonderland and catch you up on everything that you're missing out on in the Big Apple."

Wasn't this interesting timing? Her mind flitted back to the article she'd read in the medical journal last night. Her gaze turned more searching.

Had she noticed before that his smile wasn't very sincere? That his blond hair was just a bit too perfectly coiffed? Sure, he was an attractive man, but it seemed ridiculous to her now that up here in the mountains he still wouldn't risk being seen in anything less than three-hundred-dollar shoes.

Maybe it was just that seeing him here, out of context of the big city social scene, Tara could see her ex for the person he really was…a lying, cheating, social climber who was only in love with himself.

"And this is…?" Liesel injected herself into the

situation, a bona fide superwoman in Tara's eyes. She didn't know if she could do this alone.

Her ex took two of his brisk steps towards Liesel, offering her a perfectly manicured hand, "Anson Stanmore, Tara's fiancé."

"*Ex*-fiancé!" Tara sharply corrected.

Liesel sent Tara one of her raised-eyebrow looks, which she was just going to have to ignore right now.

How dared he just barge in here and start behaving like he owned her? Those days had finished the moment he'd decided to steal her research and present it as his own. Which also happened to be around the same time she'd discovered he had cheated on her not once but several times over the course of their year-long relationship. If she hadn't been neck deep in medical books and test trials maybe she would have noticed. Or—the notion suddenly struck her—maybe she hadn't wanted to notice. Maybe her heart had never really been in the relationship.

A sense of calm began to play across her frazzled nerves. Anson clearly sensed the shift as well and Tara had to suppress a smile of satisfaction as she watched him become increasingly uncomfortable under her gaze, his authority lost. *What the hell was he doing here?*

"Is there somewhere we could talk?" His eyes darted about the room as Tara eyed him coolly. "Privately?" he added, all too aware of Liesel's unabashed interest in the scene playing out before her.

"No." Tara decided to hold her ground. "Anything you have to say, you can say in front of Liesel."

Her ex's green eyes flickered nervously from the nurse to Tara. Drawing up to his full six feet, he took an impatient breath and exhaled a brusque, "Fine."

"So," Tara tapped her foot. "What can I do you for?" She intentionally borrowed Marian's folksy tone to irritate him. It appeared to work.

"Tara, quit being silly. I've come to this little backwoods outpost where you've set up camp to bring you back to New York City. Where you belong."

"I'm pretty certain New York City is the last place she belongs."

Tara's hand flew automatically to her lips at the sound of Fraser's Scottish burr.

"Fraser, I thought you were down in the Valley." Tara's heart rate quickened as she looked round to see him closing the back door behind her. He came to a stop close behind her, but his eyes were focused on her ex. Looking up at the five o'clock shadow that covered his jaw, Tara saw a muscle twitch as he clenched his jaw. It looked like Fraser and her ex weren't exactly getting off to a friendly start.

"I'm sorry." Anson put on his most insincere smile. "You are?"

"I don't think it makes a blind bit of difference who I am when you're the one who seems to be the fish out of water, mate."

Tara watched as the two men glared at each other, clearly at an impasse. She had to admit this was a completely new scenario for her. Here she was in a room with the two men who—the two men who what? One who had taught her not to trust again and one who turned her knees to jelly and just wanted to be friends. Terrific choice! At the very least, if that kiss she and Fraser had shared was anything to go by, the romance side of things with her ex could safely be consigned to the past—just a blip on her historical radar.

"Tara, you've got to be kidding me." Anson's voice turned thin. "Can't we go somewhere and talk?"

"I didn't invite you here." Tara shot Fraser a quick glance then fixed her ex with a knowing look. "You should be lucky I'm speaking to you at all."

The looks of resentment on Fraser and her ex's faces were completely undisguised. Maybe this would turn out to be quite fun! She'd never had two men jockeying for her attention before. Even if one of them "winning" her was out of the question, Tara decided to play the moment for all it was worth. Liesel was clearly enjoying herself, too. The verbal ping-pong match had just been kicked up a notch.

"Tara, I don't know what's gotten into you, but if you could peel your eyes away from your black-eyed Braveheart here for a minute, you might do me the courtesy of noticing I have made quite an effort to come out here and offer you the chance of coming back to New York, where you belong."

"Offer me the chance?" Tara's hackles had shot straight up and she didn't care who knew it. "Are you crazy?"

"I must be. Is this what you're after, Tara?" her ex shot back, gesturing first towards Fraser then grandly around the clinic. "A life with Scotland's answer to a mountain man and a bunch of skiers who don't have the cerebral wherewithal to keep themselves out of your irrelevant clinic?"

If Tara had thought her blood had run cold earlier, ice was coursing through her veins now. This had to stop. Now. There was no way Anson could speak to her like this. Not now. Not ever.

"I think you'll find the lady's quite happy here."

"Fraser, don't." Tara felt grateful for his support, but this was her battle to fight. In truth, he didn't belong here. This should've been a private conversation, but if her ex lacked the personal courtesy to be civil to her in front of Fraser, then having it out in front of her colleagues was just the way the cookie would have to crumble.

Tara turned to face the full blaze of her ex's green eyes and spoke slowly and evenly. "I am at a complete loss as to why you'd want me back in New York other than to finish the rest of *my* work in your name. I see you've run into a bit of a snag with funding. Such a shame."

She watched, gratified as the blood began to

drain from his face. Feeling a charge of confidence, she continued, "Let me tell you something I should have said long ago. You will never get your hands on a particle of my research again, particularly after the contempt you seem to have for me and the lifestyle I've chosen. I may not know much about the future, but I can assure you of one thing…" She steeled herself, knowing she was making a public declaration of independence from her old life, from the old Tara. "No matter what you say to me, you will be going back to New York City on your own."

"Hear, hear! That's my girl" Fraser couldn't help himself. This was a woman who would never cease to amaze him. He could feel it in his bones. Just look at her!

"I'm sorry?" Anson arched a furious eyebrow.

"Apologies, old boy, just couldn't keep from supporting my woman." Instinct took over and before he knew it Fraser was tipping Tara back in his arms to give her an all-consuming congratulatory kiss. A possessive kiss. A kiss being returned by Tara. One that felt promising enough to lead on to—

"What on earth do you think you're doing?"

Anson's voice broke sharply into the room and Fraser felt Tara shift her shoulders underneath the arm he now protectively placed across her shoulders.

"Just giving you a glimpse of the full picture. Tara's got everything she needs up here in Deer Creek."

"Fraser—I don't think we need to explain a thing. Perhaps you and Liesel should leave us alone to wrap this up."

Not a chance. Not with this idiot hanging around.

"I have to admit…" Tara shot her ex a wide-eyed look "…I didn't think you'd have the gall to show up here."

"Don't worry. I'm getting the message loud and clear." His green eyes darted back to Fraser before landing back on Tara with a pathetic stab at self-righteousness. "C'mon, Tara. You don't want him." Anson's voice sounded thin and whiny now. "Come back with me to New York and we'll take your work to new levels together. It's a once-in-a-lifetime opportunity."

Was he pleading with her? Seriously? Was he nuts or was she? She could see Fraser looking inquisitively at her out of her peripheral vision. She needed to wrap this up and the only way to do that was to block him out.

"If you think wasting another minute of my life for your benefit is a once-in-a-lifetime opportunity, you're crazy. C'mon, Anson, it's time to let the past stay where it belongs." *Couldn't this man take a hint?*

"Not even for a year? I'd bet you wouldn't even miss him at all—it's only a fling, right?"

"I think we're done here." Her tone was friendly, but Tara surprised herself at the level of resolve she heard in her words. She shrugged Fraser's arm from her shoulders and continued, "I belong in Deer Creek and I'm not going anywhere."

She tipped her head in Fraser's direction. "What Dr. MacKenzie does or doesn't do with his life is irrelevant to this discussion." And before either man could interject she fixed her ex with an assured eye and continued, "Let me make something very clear to you. Any research I do now or in the future will never—and I mean *never* in a million years—be done with or for you. What you did forced me to grow up and now I hold the reins in my own life. Not Fraser, not you. No one. Do you understand me?"

Anson shook his head in agreement. They were finished and he finally looked like he knew it. "I'm sorry things couldn't have worked out better for us."

"I'm not and you shouldn't be either," she responded, hoping their goodbye could also provide a much-needed closure to this chapter of their lives. "There's someone out there waiting for you and we both know it's not me."

Just saying the words sent a surge of strength through her. She was her own woman—her own woman who would decide what to do with her own life.

She watched as he turned to leave the clinic, his gait a bit too jaunty to be genuine. She couldn't help but feel a bit sorry for him and felt hugely relieved to see him leave.

A sharp draft entered the room as a twenty-something brunette escorted an ashen-faced man of about the same age through the main clinic door. She was helping him to hold his hand away from his body.

"Can you help us, please?" The woman pleaded,

oblivious to the tension in the reception area. "Allen fell on his hand and now he can't move his thumb. He's in agony."

"Absolutely." Tara gestured for the couple to enter the main examination room. "Please, come with me." She looked over at Fraser and Liesel. "Are we okay?"

Fraser answered for both of them, his eyes still firmly fixed on her ex. "Oh, don't you worry, Tara. Everything is going to be A-okay."

Tara felt about as pale as her patient looked as she closed the exam-room door firmly behind her. Long slow breaths, long slow breaths.

"Right, how can I help you?"

The man, clearly struggling with his injury, held out his hand to Tara. He flinched at her touch, explaining he'd been skiing and had fallen, "Which normally I don't do, but those snow-boarders are getting crazier every year."

"Tell me about it." Tara nodded. Remembering her first encounter with Fraser rendered her unable to stop a ripple of goosebumps from wending its way down her spine. Out of sight… She tried shaking away the images of him skimming through her head. Nope. Most certainly *not* out of mind.

"It feels as though my thumb has practically been ripped out of the socket."

"I'm not surprised." Tara forced herself to focus, completing a thorough examination of his very tender and incredibly swollen hand. "I'm afraid Mr. ..."

"Parker. Allen Parker." He filled in the blank she'd left open for him.

"I'm afraid, Mr. Parker, you've got yourself a classic case of skier's thumb."

"Skier's thumb?"

Tara smiled gently as each of the couple's eyebrows rose. They were clearly unfamiliar with the term. Good old medicine. At least she could rely on it to put her in familiar territory. Maybe she could hide here in the exam room with the Parkers for the rest of the day rather than confront Fraser about that ridiculous kiss. A flip-flop in her tummy was enough of a reminder that she had actually enjoyed that "ridiculous" kiss but even so...it had been out of order.

"Skier's thumb," she repeated, as if to prime her own memory. "It is when your thumb has

stretched or, in your case, torn the ulnar collateral ligament."

The man's pale face went gray. "That sounds
horrible!"

"It's not very nice, as you can well tell." Tara
turned to her desk to make some notes. "I would
like to take an X-ray to determine if the injury is
limited to the ligament or if a piece of bone was
pulled off when you fell. Your movement seems
fairly limited, but that could just be the swelling." She took a quick peek at the woman's ring
finger. "Mrs. Parker?"

The woman's eyes flitted to her expectantly.
Phew, got that one right. "We are going to be
a little while with X-rays and splinting up your
husband's hand."

"A splint!" Her fingers flew to her mouth,
a look of dismay passing between them. "Oh,
sweetheart. I'm so sorry."

"Don't worry, m'love. I'm the one who has gone
and messed up the vacation. Guess I'll owe you
a second run on the slopes at Valentine's Day."
They shared a kiss then, remembering Tara was
in the room, pulled apart looking slightly embar-
rassed at their spontaneous show of affection.

Tara laughed and waved off their embarrassment. "Sounds like a good solution to me!" Turning her focus to his wife, she continued, "I'm afraid you'll have to organize getting your husband's skis back to the lodge. You're staying there, right?" The couple nodded in unison.

"Perhaps if you came back in half an hour or so we'll be all wrapped up here and I'll have your husband ready for collection!"

As the couple cooed out their farewells, Tara eased herself out of the exam room, relieved to find Liesel sitting on her own at the reception desk. No sign of her ex. Good. No sign of Fraser. Not quite as good.

"Jeepers." She flicked her head in the direction of Exam One. "You'd think they were never going see each other again."

"Uh-oh. Someone's grouchy." Liesel was never afraid to call a spade a spade.

Tara huffed out a "humph" and threw an it's-hardly-surprising face over her shoulder before stomping back to the X-ray room to prepare the machines. It wasn't as if Liesel hadn't just borne witness to her life taking a seismic shift!

Her ex appears out of nowhere, just as she had

gotten her life back on track. No. That wasn't right. Her ex had been well and truly out of the picture. First, Fraser had flown into her life. Literally. Thrown everything she'd worked for over the past couple of years up into the air. But when all the pieces started to come back down, she was beginning to realize a rigidly ordered, solitary lifestyle was not necessarily what she'd been after. It was being able to trust again. The only question was, could trusting someone come in the shape of a six-foot-something Scotsman? One who literally swept her up in his arms and sent her into cloud cuckoo land with his all-too-wonderful kisses? The answer to that was a very big *no*.

Tara forced herself to count backwards from ten, exhaling a low, deep breath as the numbers slipped downwards. By the time she hit zero, a sense of calm began to unravel her tightly wound emotions. A wash of freedom suddenly flooded through her as if the last bit of weight tethering her to her past had finally been lifted.

She was in charge. Not Anson, not Fraser.

Fraser... She would have to make it clear to him that she could fight her own battles. A smile began to play at the corners of her lips. Seeing Anson's face after Fraser had kissed her had been priceless. Maybe she did owe him a thank you. A little one. And a reprimand. Stealing kisses was most assuredly not in his contract.

But it would have to wait. It had been a busy day already and, with numbers increasing on the slopes, patients were coming in at a steady rate. Which was just what she needed right now. Work. Focus. And absolutely no men.

CHAPTER SIX

"Room for one more?"

The look on Tara's face told Fraser that waiting for an answer wouldn't be a good idea. He slipped onto the chairlift beside her and carried on talking as if she'd given him a broad smile of welcome. "I saw you heading for the slopes and thought I'd make good on that race I promised you."

"If you were really going to make good on the promise, you would've shown up yesterday."

"She shoots, she scores!" Fraser called out cheerily. Tara turned away silently from him and fixed her gaze on the ski lift's path. *Ouch.*

Suddenly the lift ride didn't seem long enough to make a dent in Tara's mood. She was doing a stellar job of pretending they weren't sitting thigh to thigh, floating up a mountainside together as the dawn light poured over the ridges of Deer Creek. Her dark curls peeped out from under her red bobbled ski hat and it was all Fraser could do not to lift up a gloved finger and tuck one behind her ear.

A different tack was needed as the comedy approach was meeting a dead end in the results department. This whole stop-start friendship thing needed to be fixed. He was pretty sure they both needed a bit of "even keel". *Here goes nothing.*

"I think I may have overstepped the mark yesterday. Put my foot in it, so to speak."

"Which foot was that? Your right or left?" She looked appraisingly at him, suddenly appearing to enjoy watching him squirm. "Or both?"

"Probably both if it manifests itself as acting like a jealous boyfriend."

Tara laughed away the comment nervously. Fraser's timing was awful. Perfectly awful. *Or awfully perfect?* They needed to address the elephant on the chair lift. He was obviously trying to make an effort and she hardly needed to be churlish to prove her point. The new improved Tara was ready for action.

"In fairness, you probably did me a favor."

Fraser gave her a nod to continue. "When you ki— What you did probably helped my ex understand my life is well and truly different—that *I* am well and truly different." She pulled her eyes away from his and returned them to the slopes, "Even if it wasn't an entirely accurate portrayal of things."

Having that muscular thigh pressing against her own was hardly a foolproof method of blocking out Fraser's stab at being a Cro-Magnon yesterday. She could hardly tell Fraser that kissing him again had had the same knee-weakening effect it had had the first time. If romance wasn't completely off limits he would definitely be her perfect choice.

Perfect? What was that anyhow? If her life had been a picture-perfect snow globe a few weeks ago she had little doubt who had come and shaken it all up. She looked up at the sky, snowflakes landing softly on her lashes. *Ease up, Tara. There are worse things in life than a man trying to protect your honor.*

"What I'm trying to say is thanks and don't worry about it. We're good. That man manages to bring out the worst in everyone." She shot Fraser a horrified look. "Not that you were at your worst. I mean…it was nice what you did.

The intent anyway…not necessarily the execution. But—"

"Tara, stop. It's all right." Fraser laid a gloved finger on her lips. A soothing contrast to the rigid commands she was used to receiving from her ex. More like a *sexy* contrast!

"Why don't we just start with a clean slate?" He pointed to the snow gently falling around them. "Pure as the driven snow?"

Her cheeks went rosy. Traitors! Her thoughts since his arrival had been far from pure. She'd have to work on that.

"Deal." She nodded in the direction of the dismount platform as the lift neared the top of the black diamond run. "It looks like you're going to have an opportunity to prove yourself right about now."

"I think we must've had two new feet of snow overnight!" Liesel stood at the window of the clinic reception area, eyes sparkling at the prospect of cutting some fresh tracks into the morning's untouched slopes.

"Go on." Tara waved a hand in the direction of the front doors. "Go have a ski if you like. Fraser and I had a good run this morning and I only need you back before the novices start running into new-powder problems."

"You and Fraser had a sunrise run?"

"It was nothing, Liesel." She waggled a warning finger at her friend. "Just two colleagues having a friendly race."

"I'll bet it was friendly." Liesel's eyes danced merrily.

"Go on—get out of here now before I change my mind."

"Are you sure?"

"Positive. If you wait until this afternoon, the runs will be covered in crud and you've more than earned a bit of fresh-powder time."

Tara grinned as Liesel skipped out of the clinic. Her ski vocabulary had come a long way since she'd moved to Deer Creek. Not to mention her skills on the slopes. Despite the heavy snow overnight, she'd managed to trounce Fraser soundly that morning. It had been an exhilarating run down her favorite piste.

After making her agree to a rematch the next morning, Fraser had headed back to the lifts for another few runs while she opened the clinic.

He wasn't rostered on until later in the day and vowed to get his revenge.

In between patients, Tara checked her laptop to see if the roads were clear. When she called the lodge reception desk they confirmed her ex had checked out. Letting a heavy exhalation whoosh through her lips, she was surprised at how good she felt.

He had left the clinic knowing his place in her life now—absolutely nowhere. And clearing the slate with Fraser had felt good. She felt grown up—womanly.

A grown woman. A doctor, for heaven's sake! A doctor who was having a whale of a time up here in Deer Creek where the snow fell thick and fast. Christmas was practically around the corner and, most importantly, her patients were treated with the high level of care they deserved. The clinic was just a few months away from being her own private practice. A small inheritance from her parents meant she had already been able to partially buy out the previous doctor, who'd decided he'd had enough snow and moved to Hawaii. The resort owned the rest of it for now. By spring, it would all be hers.

She just needed to maintain her focus. Not let Fraser and those mind-boggling kisses of his get to her. There was no chance she was going to give up all of this just because her heart was turning some fairly wild somersaults.

A flush of heat began to creep up her cheeks at the memory of exactly why her heart was cartwheeling around her ribcage. She closed her eyes for a moment, realizing too late how easy it was to transport herself back to that first magical moment. There she was, standing between Fraser's legs as he pulled her in close...

"A latte for the doc?"

Tara's eyes flew open. Yup! It was Mr. Perfect Timing slipping her favorite hot drink across the counter.

"I thought you were busy trying to improve your race time."

"There was so little to improve, I did it in the next run," he countered with a broad smile.

"I'll believe that when I see it."

"You're on. Dawn still early enough for you?"

"Again." Tara sent him a doubting look despite the smile playing across her lips, "I'll believe that when I see it."

"You've got to learn to let bygones be bygones, my dear." He sent her a slow wink and tapped the side of his still slightly bruised nose. "Let me start my shift early to make up for it."

"Fair enough." Tara picked up the coffee he'd brought her and took a long warming draft. He was right. She needed to learn to let go a bit more. Trust. A lot easier said than done.

Fraser took a full swig of his latte and immediately pulled a face. Stone cold. That afternoon the clinic had seen back-to-back patients. Even when Liesel had joined them, they had been run off of their feet. Fraser was energized by the work, happy to have somewhere to focus his energies. A fresh snowfall was a big lure to skiers. The new powder was easier on the knees and covered over hazardous runs that could have become icy overnight from too much compaction. But a new layer of snow, particularly one this deep, had its own set of hazards.

Skiers unfamiliar with the resort wouldn't know which paths to stick to, and cross-country skiers were often tempted to go well beyond what would have been a safe distance. The worst case the ski patrol had seen that morning had been what could have very easily been a tree-well suffocation. A twenty-something snowboarder had been racing down a black diamond run and fallen head first into a tree well, becoming immobilized. If it hadn't been for his fast-thinking friends, whistling and calling the ski patrol for help, he might very well be dead now.

As Fraser soberly signed the young man out of the clinic after an obligatory health check, he reminded him that ninety percent of people involved in tree-well falls were suffocated. "If you can, thrill-seek safely," he called after him as the clinic doors swung shut.

Good advice. Could he apply it to kissing a beautiful American woman when he had no intention of staying?

Fraser had barely seen Tara since he'd arrived that morning. Each of them were kept busy in separate examination rooms as patients arrived presenting with minor head injuries, a couple of broken wrists, several skiers' thumbs and a particularly painful-looking patella or kneecap dislocation. He'd felt so badly for the poor young girl he'd carried her back to the lodge as her mother had towed her snowboard behind them. The mountains could be so much fun, but a healthy degree of caution was definitely called for when whizzing along the slopes.

As he returned to the clinic, Fraser caught himself sending a sharp laugh out into the crisp afternoon air. The pithy words of wisdom he dispensed to his patients could very easily apply to his private life. Perhaps there was a way he could superimpose one of those warning signs on Tara every time he looked at that tempting pair of lips of hers. *Rein it in, Fraser. It'll all soon be over and before you know it Tara will be but a distant memory.* He sucked in another lungful of biting mountain air. *At least that's what you've got to keep telling yourself.*

Tara let herself into her apartment, relieved the day was over. It had been three weeks since she'd had the showdown with her ex and mercifully things at the clinic had been so busy she'd had remarkably little time to think about how much had changed since the arrival of one Dr. Fraser MacKenzie.

Allowing herself to slump down onto the bench

of her kitchen nook, she shrugged off her coat where she sat.

Sliding her radio into the center of the table, Tara double-checked the receiver was in the "on" position. After being caught out those few weeks ago, she had been doubly careful the radio was always functioning. The lifts had been closed for the day, but occasionally at night the radio crackled to life. Cross-country skiers caught out by bad weather, a slip and fall in the parking lot. Nothing too outrageous had happened over the past year, but she'd heard stories and definitely wanted to be prepared.

There was more snow forecast for that night and, even though it wasn't technically her responsibility, if anyone took ill at the lodge she was more than happy to go over and check them out.

It was funny, she noted, looking around her kitchen. She'd always been perfectly happy to come home to her little bachelorette apartment. Happy to potter around, read a book, do some research, watch a little television. Now, with Fraser's arrival, her time alone felt quiet in a different way. Emptier. Her early morning runs down the Elk Slip now felt incomplete if he didn't show.

He was there most mornings and—in fairness—if he didn't show he left a note at the clinic or called her the night before to tell her not to wait for him. More trips to the Valley. He must have really hit it off with the hospital staff down there. Which was a good thing. Right?

Blowing a sigh through her lightly parted lips, she leant her head back against the wall. In truth, she'd really enjoyed the past few weeks. Fraser was an excellent doctor and she felt they had each made strides professionally. Sharing tips and anecdotes from various cases, each day served as confirmation that the pair of them worked well together. That they made a good team. Professionally, of course. If only she could just stop the butterflies tracking the course of her entire insides each time she was near him, getting through the season would be a whole lot easier.

Letting her head fall into her crossed arms on the table, Tara allowed herself a small whimper of despair. They were only a few weeks into the first of the winter snow and she was already dreading the end of it. Fraser had probably booked tickets to go on to some other resort on the other side of the world in the spring. She would be a whole lot better off coming to terms with his eventual departure now. Unless…

Was there anything here in Deer Creek she could use to keep him here?

She racked her brain. A dozen of Marian's blueberry muffins weekly for life? Possibly.

A membership to the valley golf club? Doctors liked golf, didn't they? Scottish ones in particular. She thought for a moment before sending a barely audible "uh-uh" into the still air of her apartment. She didn't play golf at all and suspected Fraser, a man who chased snow around the globe, wasn't a big fan either. Back to muffins.

An offer of a free massage every week? Nope. Definitely not. Too dangerous.

She pushed herself up from the table and plodded into the bathroom. It was a pointless exercise. Fraser was a man who liked change. One glimpse at his résumé had told her that.

And she liked her privacy. Privacy and friendship. Friendship was precisely what she wanted with the sexiest, most spine-tinglingly gorgeous man she'd ever seen. Yessirree!

Tara twisted the taps open on the bath and a

nice whoosh of steam began to fill the bathroom. Maybe a double dose of bubbles would help.

Tara groaned as she heard the radio crackle to life just five minutes into her relaxing bath.

"This is Ski Rescue One to Dr. Tara Braxton. Do you read me? Over." Tara leapt out of the bath, nearly slipping on the floor and cracking her head on the doorframe in the process. Pulling a thick red towel around herself, she lurched into the kitchen and grabbed the radio, water pooling at her feet.

Trying not to sound too breathless, she pushed the button on the side of the radio and responded with her call numbers.

"Dr. Braxton, this is your social medic demanding your presence at the Blue Lantern Tavern for Peanut Night. Over."

Tara smiled at the radio as she belatedly recognized her colleague's Australian accent. She swiped at some bubbles bobbling on her shoulder. Ski Medic One was Eric's call name. With the pair being inseparable outside work hours, it was little wonder how Liesel had gotten hold of the radio. "Ski Medic One, I think you can get through the night on your own." She took a glimpse out of the window and saw the air was laced with fat snowflakes. A cozy night in by the fire would be just fine. Honestly.

"Dr. Braxton, declining our invitation is not an option. Snowmobile will be at your stairs for pick-up in five minutes. Over."

Tara laughingly tried to reply, but knew Liesel well enough. The nurse would have turned off her radio and, like it or not, her chauffeur-driven snowmobile would be there in a few minutes. Peanut Night at the Blue was an institution at Deer Creek—not just for the locals but for the seasonal rescue crews and medics. After the lifts had shut on a Sunday night, a good crowd of merrymakers would go to the bar to listen to music and share pitchers of beer over bottomless baskets of salty peanuts whose shells you could just toss on the floor.

Some nights it was a mellow affair and others? Well, Tara had only heard about how wild things could get at the Blue. She'd always managed to sneak out before things had gotten too crazy. Tonight, to keep Liesel happy, she would have a beer or two, maybe brave a game of darts and then slip out when no one was watching.

"You don't look ready to go."

Tara froze, the towel barely clutched round her. The all-too-familiar Scottish brogue unleashed a ripple of pleasure shimmying around her insides. Why was that voice coming from her kitchen door?

Because none other than Fraser MacKenzie was standing at her kitchen door, that's why.

"What on earth...?"

"Liesel radioed me and said you'd asked for me to come by and collect you for something called peanut night." Tara pursed her lips. Of course she had. Nice one, Liesel. *Guess you've joined ranks with Marian in playing cupid.* She'd only just managed to feel as if the "friends thing" could work with Fraser. She hadn't had a chance to test the theory in a social setting. Terrific!

"Am I early?" He carried on speaking through the door's glass window as if it was perfectly normal to stand on someone's porch on a Sunday night while they dripped bath oil and bubbles onto their kitchen floor.

"Just a little." Tara stepped to the door and

flipped the lock open, all too aware of the heat creeping up her neck. She was practically stark naked in front of the man she'd had more than one colorful thought about. Not really the way she'd imagined him seeing her. Not that she'd imagined *that* or anything.

"Give me five minutes, will you?" Without waiting for a reply, she raced off to her bedroom, ensuring the door was closed. Tight. She was going to kill Liesel when she saw her.

A couple of minutes of frenzied drying and clothes-grabbing later, Tara let herself fall back onto her bed as she wiggled into a pair of fresh-from-the-dryer jeans. Thank goodness it was poorly lit in the Blue, she thought with a smirk as she slipped the button snugly into place. Rattling through her shirts, Tara chose a loose-checked cotton top with long sleeves she knew hung well on her shoulders. The Blue was hardly dressy, but she joined in the peanut nights so rarely she may as well make a small effort. Looking good for Fraser had nothing to do with it.

Liar.

A quick glance in the mirror revealed that steaming in the bath had brought out a soft curl in the tendrils of hair that had escaped from her hastily clipped coif. *That'll work.* A bit of mascara and a squirt of her favorite perfume completed the job.

Rummaging through the bottom of her closet, she found a pair of cowboy boots she'd picked up when she'd first moved to Deer Creek. She ran an appreciative hand over the well-tooled leatherwork. They had cost far more than she'd planned on spending, but surely a new beginning in a mountain resort had been more than enough reason to splash out on a pair of boots that would show her intent to stay?

All too aware Fraser was twiddling his thumbs in the kitchen, Tara relinquished a few more minutes in front of her vanity in favor of ending the awkward encounter. She pulled on her thick leather coat, flicking the woolen collar up around her neck. If Fraser had seen her practically naked ten minutes ago, he was going to see her over-clothed now. Shaking her head as she left her room, she had to laugh. Liesel was a rare breed. There weren't that many people who could get out of a soothing bubble bath and

into a bar full of rowdy ski patrollers in under
ten minutes.

"Your carriage awaits, m'lady!"

Tara was grateful Fraser seemed just as willing as
she was to gloss over the fact he'd just seen a bit
more of her than either of them had bargained on.
Her already frayed nerves jangled with a combination of fear and anticipation. She was all too
aware that the safest way to ride on the back of
the snowmobile was behind Fraser with her arms
around him. It didn't help that he was looking
particularly gorgeous in the twinkling Christmas lights she'd put up on the stairwell leading
to her porch. A thick blue turtleneck the color
of his eyes met his well-defined jaw, and snowflakes gathered on his dark woolen hat. *Winter
wonderland, indeed.*

"It's only a fifteen-minute walk from here,"
she stalled, her body betraying her by tingling
with desire.

"And on this…" Fraser lowered his rich voice
and waggled his eyebrows "…it will only be
five."

Tara raised a wary eyebrow.

"C'mon, darlin'." He put on a hokey cowboy accent as he registered her obvious hesitation. "Jump aboard my horse and hold on tight."

Tara's body was screaming at her to get a move on. The living, breathing image of her fantasy man was standing right in front of her, beckoning her to snuggle up to him on a beautiful wintry evening. Not a good idea if you want to keep things platonic.

Uh-oh. Body is overriding brain again.

Tara slipped a leg over the saddle of the snowmobile, her arms automatically wrapping around Fraser's waist.

Okay. Good. I can do this. Not a single problem in the world, sitting here with my arms wrapped around Fraser MacKenzie, my good friend and colleague.

Actually…she felt herself wriggle in a little closer. This wasn't bad. Not bad at all. Normally, she felt quite tall and awkward, but with Fraser's height and build she caught herself feeling ridiculously feminine as her body molded just a bit more closely against his. Even her fingers felt dainty and ladylike as she slipped her mittened hands a bit further round Fraser's waist. It was all she could do not to nestle her head into his shoulder, cuddling up to him as though they were a couple who had been together for years. Fraser turned his head to the side, not making eye contact. His husky voice made it clear he was as aware as she was of their physical connection.

"Hang on, love. You're in for one helluva ride."

Fraser had to will himself to concentrate. Safe delivery of Tara to the Blue Lantern was his first priority. His second was ensuring she didn't realize just how sexy it felt having her arms wrapped around him, her legs streamlined against his own. Even her breath played on his neck like the silent call of a sensual siren. He'd never seen anyone make an oversized leather jacket and a pair of cowboy boots look so suggestive. Keeping things platonic with this woman was going to be harder than finishing med school had been. Hell, boot camp had been easier than keeping his level of arousal in check.

Fraser would've felt perfectly happy forgoing the trip to the bar and instead spending the evening driving up and down the tiny main street all night long. Snowflakes sparkled in the Christmas lights that had been put up over the past couple of weeks. Nothing garish, just string after string of multicolored bulbs hung like garlands between the buildings. A few hundred yards further along, you could just make out the lodge, fairy lights tastefully outlining the gables and windows.

It was little wonder Tara had chosen this place after New York. Whatever had happened between her and her ex was none of his business, but feeling Tara press her body up against his as they rode through the magical winterscape… of all the people who deserved a thank-you card right now it had to be her ex.

Fraser kept the speed of the snowmobile steady, forsaking the usual macho route of the-man-on-fast-motorized-beast. Keeping it steady drew out the journey just a couple of exquisite minutes longer. Once they got to the bar, chances were pretty slim he wouldn't get to be this close to her, and if a five-minute ride became six or seven, where was the harm?

All too soon, the glow of a neon blue lantern appeared through the mist of snowflakes and cloud settling around the resort.

Wanting to ensure he'd get a bit more time with

Tara tonight, Fraser decided to lay his cards on the table. Well, some of his cards. No one got the full deck.

"I hope you're not going to abandon me to the locals when we get in here."

Tara chuckled as she pulled herself off of the snowmobile. "I don't know. They're a pretty vicious group. You might have to be the one to protect me."

She didn't need to ask twice. "You can count on me." At least for now.

He wondered if she was as aware of his touch as he was of touching her. It felt nice. The whole scenario was good. Familiar. Arriving together. It would've been perfectly natural to weave his fingers through hers and enter the bar hand in hand. He toyed with the idea of allowing himself just one night off from their "just friends" pact.

He allowed himself to watch her as she kicked the snow off her boots on the side of the Blue's porch. Her cheeks were flushed with the cold of the night, face framed in a swirl of soft curls, lips a deeper red than he'd imagined possible.

Nope. Can't go there.

Entering the bar was the only way to regain

control. Fraser skipped up the steps of the bar onto the broad wooden porch. Pulling open the thick wooden door, he ushered Tara in ahead of him, resisting the urge to slip a protective hand on the small of her back. They were hit with a blast of warm air, country music, co-mingled scents of beer, burgers and fries, and most of all laughter.

"What a great place!" Fraser enthused.

"It's not your typical Scottish pub, is it?" Tara smiled up at him. Going up on tiptoe, she fought against the music to be heard, "What's your poison?"

You.

"Do you know a good local beer on tap?"

"I like the apricot ale, but a lot of the guys think it's too girly and prefer Grizzly Stout. Do you like that sort of thing?"

As long as it comes attached to a five-foot-nine-inch doctor who doesn't have the slightest clue just how beautiful she is.

"I trust your judgment."

He watched as Tara wove her way through the crowd, oblivious to the appreciative smiles and glances being thrown her way by more than one ski patroller and off-duty hotel staffer. A low whistle of admiration escaped his lips. She just oozed class. Even in a peanut-shell-covered bar with little more than a dartboard and pool table for decoration. Pure class.

"And that's how we roll!"

Tara gave Liesel a high five after the nurse neatly pocketed the eight ball. Eric sent Fraser a "hard luck" look from across the table, clearly aware he was dating Deer Creek's resident pool shark. Tara wasn't half-bad either.

"Why didn't you tell me you were a grifter?"

Tara pushed out her lower lip and shrugged with an it-was-nothing gesture, all too unaware of the effect it had on him. "I've had a bit of time to practice. Peanut Night tends to be the only thing that gets me out on a Sunday night."

"I'll have to remember that." Fraser stuffed his hands in his pockets, hoping to hide the sensations shotputting through him as visions of leaning down and nibbling away at Tara's lower lip ran through his head.

"What else gets you out and about?"

"Well…" Tara pulled herself up onto a stool,

grabbing a peanut and flicking the shell in half with her thumb. "I have to admit I haven't been to the ER lately—down at Valley Hospital—and I quite enjoy my time there."

"What about it exactly?" Fraser was intrigued, and not just with watching Tara pop peanuts into her mouth. Every time she took a sip of beer the tip of her tongue would take a little run over her top lip to catch any stray foam. *Very distracting.* He would have to stop staring at her mouth and focus on their conversation. In truth, the more he knew Tara, the more he wanted to know everything there was to know about her. It was a rare breed of doctor who didn't get burnt out by long runs in the hospital emergency room. Yet another attribute he could chalk up to her growing list.

"Well, not to sound selective, because helping any patient is worth my while, but the ER is the perfect location to see patients coming in with compound fractures and other bone conditions. As you know, I had been doing a lot of research—"

She suddenly stopped speaking, her eyes clouding with emotion.

"You were doing research..." Fraser repeated, hoping she'd continue.

Tara bit at her lower lip, her eyes committed to inspecting her empty beer glass before she looked up suddenly with a flash of parted lips and white teeth. She had a cheeky smile. It was nice to see.

"You know enough about me and I know next to nothing about you. Let's talk about all your dark secrets!"

The crack of pain Tara saw flash across Fraser's eyes was gone in an instant. But she had seen it. She felt a twist of compassion in her stomach as she searched his sapphire eyes for answers. There was so much more to this man than a carefree playboy on a quest to hit all the high peaks of the world. She'd hit more than a nerve. She knew it—and yet it looked as if she would never be able to unlock that part of him that seemed to hurt so much...

"C'mon." She impulsively took his hand in hers. "Let's dance!"

Several couples were out on the hardwood floor, swept clear of peanut shells, getting into place for a bit of a slipshod line dancing. The band that'd been playing quiet country songs throughout the evening gave each other some sort of silent signal and before she knew it Tara found herself being swept along to "Honky Tonk Badonkadonk" with the rest of the couples.

Looking across the dance floor, she was impressed to see that Fraser was keeping up with the complicated series of steps far better than she was. She may not be learning his dark secrets, but she was certainly discovering the man could move on a dance floor. Thankfully, it was easy not to feel self-conscious as the ramshackle collection of regulars and out-of-towners were hardly contenders for America's finest line dancers, but even so she found herself hoping Fraser didn't notice her two left feet.

The combination of music and a genuinely warm atmosphere soon had Tara dissolving into fits of giggles. She really was a disaster on the dance floor. If this had been New York, she would've felt humiliated and, no doubt, would have found herself being chastised by her ex for behaving so freely in public. Here, with Fraser, she felt like anything in the world was possible.

What had started as a quiet—no, lonely—evening at home had turned into a remarkably fun night. Catching Fraser's eye was easy. His warm gaze hadn't left her all evening. At least, that was how he made her feel. As she started to sway quietly in time to a slow song the band had just begun to play, Tara felt herself being slammed with a jolt of passion so intense she couldn't have imagined it possible. Fraser wasn't even touching her, wasn't near her, and yet her skin felt as though it were virtually alight with sensation.

As if being magnetically pulled to him, she crossed the dance floor, barely avoiding couples rocking side to side in one another's arms. She felt his arms slip around her waist and pull her firmly into his hips. Her arms rested briefly on his and she allowed herself one, maybe two heavy-lidded moments to savor the warm scent emanating from his chest. An aching hunger for him turned her knees into putty and wrapping her arms up and around his neck was the only way she could manage to stay upright. Everyone around them seemed to dissolve into a distant blur, as if she were in a film, fading away from the dance floor, aware of the privacy of the moment being shared.

Tara tilted her chin up and felt Fraser's cheek,

rough with stubble, meet her own. A wash of heat cascaded through her. Her body responded primally. Every moment that passed seemed to last in a luxurious rush of sensation. Just the slightest of movements and she would be able to taste his lips again. They'd be delicious and male and so very much what she had been avoiding. Intimacy. Her every thought was a rule-breaker. It wasn't even her style. Kissing in public, in such a small town. Not that it had stopped her from responding to the kiss Fraser had given her in front of her ex.

Who was she kidding? Small town or big town, her ex was gone and her feelings for Fraser were a totally separate issue. She was drawn to him and yet everything about him screamed, *Don't trust him!* Why, oh, why, was she having this very public reaction to dancing in his arms? Her entire body ached with longing.

Please stay. I know it's crazy, but couldn't you just stay?

She felt Fraser tip his head towards hers and his lips brushed along her neck, sending a visible shudder down the length of her spine. "We've got plenty of time, love. Plenty of time."

Fraser tightened his grip on her waist, gently releasing one of her clasped hands from his neck and holding it firmly, decisively against his chest. She hoped he couldn't feel the rapid pounding of her heart as she allowed herself to nestle into him, gently swaying to the music.

Her mind was racing—the antithesis of their slow, rhythmic swaying. *What was he saying?* Her initial impressions that he was a love-'em-and-leave-'em type hadn't held up over the past few weeks. He'd been an excellent colleague and a good friend too.

It was time to face reality. Not everyone was like her ex—there to use her until she wasn't of value any more. Not everyone smelled so incredibly good. Or felt so good. Right here, right now.

Risking a glimpse up at Fraser's face, she was rewarded with a small kiss on her forehead. The pleasurable thrill that ran through her pulled her thoughts into sharper focus.

Just enjoy the moment. This may not last, but just enjoy the moment.

CHAPTER SEVEN

TARA STAMPED HER feet and gave her mittened hands a brisk rub. *Where was he?* She'd been waiting for Fraser for over ten minutes and, with the sun long gone, the temperatures were dropping fast. No matter how much she reasoned with herself that he was just a colleague, every time they organized to meet, her nerves flew into giddy overdrive. She wished she'd not been so silly and worried about a knitted hat messing up her hair. It wasn't as if she was going on a date with him or anything. Not really. Just a couple of colleagues meeting some other ER doctors for a friendly bowling night down in the Valley.

She watched as another gondola made its steady journey down to the Valley. Cold or not, it was absolutely beautiful up here. The viewing deck offered a one-eighty-degrees display of Christmas lights twinkling away in the distance. If Fraser got his act together and showed up they

could be in amongst the festive decorations—and warmth!

"It's pretty amazing up here, isn't it?"

Tara whirled around just in time to receive the full effect of another one of those butterfly-inducing smiles. *This is not a date. This is not a date!*

A week had passed since she and Fraser had spent those few precious minutes with their arms wrapped around each other on the dance floor. Despite her best efforts she still hadn't managed to shake off her body's primal reaction to him. Little wonder since he always looked like he could be stepping off the pages of some sports magazine or another.

Even so, sticking to the "just friends" routine had made it easier to see him every day at work. And a little bit harder. It wasn't as if she wasn't tempted, but getting to know him had remained as impossible a task as it been from the start. He was great at asking her questions about herself, but always managed to change the topic deftly whenever she tried to swing their conversations round to his past. Still, they had started meeting regularly on the slopes for an early morning run and a chaser of Marian's blueberry pancakes to go over any business they needed to discuss before opening the clinic. It was a fun routine and she'd miss it when he was gone.

The butterflies whirling around her stomach landed with a thump. She didn't want to think about that day. Not yet.

"Hope you haven't been waiting too long."

"No, not at all. I've just been enjoying the lights." *Fibber.* Why are you speaking to him like he's some sort of brand-new acquaintance? *C'mon, Tara, you've surely passed the awkward chitchat phase?*

She looked up at him, enjoying the blanket of twinkling lights spread out before them. Here he was, right next to her—so close and yet she suddenly felt as though she was staring at a stranger. What kept him from sharing his history with her? In their short time together Fraser had shown an unerring ability to draw her own story from her. It made her feel as if the relationship was...not one-sided exactly, but as if she could be doing something more to let Fraser know he'd be just as safe telling her about his past. If one thing was certain, she knew he would never take advantage of her the way her ex had. Fraser had too much character, was laced at the seams with a sense of compassionate duty.

She crossed her fingers within the secret confines of her mittens. *Please, don't let him think spending time with me is a duty.*

She watched her breath collect in little clouds, not wanting to chance another look up into those lake-blue eyes of his.

"I haven't been on the gondola before—how long does it take?" His baritone slipped naturally into the wintry silence.

"Ooh—not long, from memory. It's been awhile since I've gone down on the gondola."

"I thought you did a shift at the hospital last week."

Well remembered. Keeping tabs on me, eh? "I got a ride down from Eric." Fraser lifted an enquiring eyebrow. "He had a training course down at the hospital so said he'd take me."

They turned simultaneously at the sound of a family approaching the gondola viewing platform. Tara felt a small twitch of relief. *That takes care of the problem of being on a twenty-minute ride all on our own...*

"How are he and Liesel getting on?" Fraser let a mischievous smile play upon his lips, his eyes twinkling.

"I don't think I need to answer that one." Tara gave a snort of laughter despite herself. "It would take a blind person not to see they are head over heels for each other." She quickly lowered her eyes, not wanting Fraser to see even a glimmer of yearning for the same happiness the pair exuded. If ever there was a picture-book version of falling in love, what Liesel and Eric had going on was definitely it. They had even started finishing each other's sentences. She was so very happy for them, but also felt questions teasing away at her own resolve to stay a lone she-wolf.

"Here we are." She felt Fraser's hand slip onto the small of her back as the gondola approached. The knot of nerves weighing down her core unfurled in a delicious twist of heat. *This is not a date. This is not a date.*

"You know I've never done this before, right?" Fraser lifted the bowling ball from the rack and gave Tara what he hoped was some approximation of a wide-eyed innocent. Surely throwing a twelve-pound sparkling purple ball down a wooden lane wouldn't be that big a challenge. He'd had military training, for crying out loud! Fraser stopped at the sound of a loud buzzer and Tara's uninhibited laughter.

"You can't step over that line, you big picklehead!"

"Picklehead? What sort of a slight is that? Surely you can come up with something better." Fraser joined in Tara's infectious laughter, silently admitting he had been distracted from the start of their game. He and Tara had arrived late and had been assigned to a lane together. Each time she went up to collect a ball and send it hurtling down the lane, he only had eyes for her slender form bending, leaning, fluidly holding a pose in line with the bowling ball's trajectory. It was all incredibly distracting. She was distracting.

Thank goodness they had all agreed to switch partners after a couple of games. There was no chance he was going to make any sort of headway with Tara bewitching his limited skill right out of the bowling alley.

Fraser sent the ball on what initially looked like a long-hoped-for straight shot down the center of the lane when, at the last moment, it careened off to the side and landed with a *thunk* in the alley.

"My turn again!" Tara's voice was positively gleeful. He couldn't help but give her a playful knock with his shoulder as he made his way back to the scoring table. Pool shark and now a bowling champion. What other little tricks did she have up her sleeve?

He collapsed into the chair she'd vacated to watch her lean forward with a studied concentration. Arm back, body poised and, whoosh—she unleashed the scarlet bowling ball into the lane with a practiced swing.

"No-o-o-o!" She'd done it again! Another strike. Unbelievable. Nor was that beautiful smile on her lips. What he wouldn't give to deserve the chance to kiss them every single—

"You two ready to make a switch?" Fraser looked up at the approaching player—one of the guys he'd met when he'd done a shift in the ER a couple of weeks ago. "You'd better watch yourself if you're taking on Tara. She's a menace." Fraser stood as Tara approached. He couldn't stop himself from throwing what he hoped looked like a casually draped arm around her shoulder. He wasn't marking his territory. Not exactly.

A pretty brunette appeared at the ER doctor's elbow, raising herself up on tiptoe to give his cheek a kiss before putting a hand forward to introduce herself to Fraser.

"I'm Jane. From what I've seen, I had better play Tara next—I think you two would be better suited to one another." She nodded at her boyfriend—was it Ryan?

"Why's that? Is he as good at gutter balls as I am?" Fraser chanced a wink and a smile at Tara.

"Better!" the brunette parried on her boyfriend's behalf. Fraser felt Tara wriggle herself out from underneath his arm.

"Anyone fancy a beer or something before the next game?" Tara linked arms with Jane before Fraser had a chance to offer to go up to the snack bar with her.

Looked like he'd overstepped the mark. Again.

"Just a soda for me," he called to her back as she disappeared into the crowd. Fraser turned back toward the lanes, pulling a hand through his hair. Was this the four- or five-millionth time he'd put his foot wrong with this woman?

"Don't worry, man. We've all tried." Ryan gave Fraser a friendly pat on the shoulder.

Fraser couldn't keep his puzzled expression at bay. "Tried what?"

"You know." He tipped his head in the direction Tara was heading, "Tried to date Tara."

Fraser took a step back and laughed, grateful Ryan couldn't read his thoughts right now. Ready. Aim. Fire and bullseye! Crikey. He didn't think he was that transparent.

"Don't worry, mate. It's nothing like that at all," Fraser quickly covered. "We've just got a really good working relationship that seems to have blossomed into…" Into what exactly? A flirtation without expectations? Hardly. The woman set his whole nerve center into overdrive. "A good friendship," he finished solidly, knowing full well he was on shaky ground.

"Sure, pal." Ryan gave him another amiable clap on the shoulder before settling onto one of the orange plastic players' chairs.

"Honestly, we really enjoy working together!" Fraser knew he was veering a bit too close to "the gentleman doth protest too much" territory.

Ryan leant forward, elbows on his knees, looking as though he was a coach about to deliver a *you can do it* speech to his rookie quarterback. "Look, Fraser, you seem like a nice guy, but a word to the wise—the little I know about Tara Braxton is that her life is her work and there is no, and I mean *no*, room for romance in it."

"And what's wrong with that exactly?"

Ryan sat back in his chair, looking surprised at Fraser's response.

"Nothing, if that's your gig."

"She's a very dedicated doctor and has a lot to give to the medical world."

Ryan raised his hands up in a surrender pose. "Hey, man, I'm not trying to pick a fight. I just thought...you know..." His eyes worked their way back to the snack bar, where Tara stood laughing with Jane, then returned to Fraser with one of those wink, wink, nudge, nudge looks.

"No." Fraser needed to nip this one in the bud. "Just friends. That's it."

"That's cool. I have to admit. I'm a little bit jealous."

Easily understood. "Of what?"

"We did a couple of internet searches on her a couple of times after her volunteer shifts at the

ER and when it comes to orthopedics, talk about impressive."

Fraser felt himself smiling proudly, as if he'd had the slightest thing to do with Tara's medical knowledge. Ryan continued, oblivious to Fraser's internal monologue. "We are just surprised she hasn't come to us to carry on with her research here. Especially now that the intellectual rights are up for grabs."

Fraser leapt at the suggestion, even though it wasn't his to take. "You know about that? Her research?"

"Sure." Ryan pressed his hands to his legs and stood up. "We all do. The wonderful world of orthopedics isn't that big and let me tell you—I'm surprised you didn't hear a cheer coming from the hospital when we heard her ex got what was coming to him. He completely deceived her and now it sounds like a big slice of karma pie has landed on his plate. Serves him right." Ryan ambled over to the ball rack and selected a blue twelve-pounder. Fraser's mind was reeling with possibilities. Possibilities on a very close horizon. Tara could continue her research. Right here!

Ryan looked over his shoulder at Fraser as he

headed towards the lane. "Don't quote me on this, but over at the hospital the rumor is that if she wanted to use our place as a launch pad, all she has to do is say the word."

CHAPTER EIGHT

"Is IT ALL right if I take off early today?" Liesel twisted a curl of red hair expertly into place, returning her pixie cut to a picture of perfection. "Eric's promised to take me down to the Valley for a movie if the roads aren't too bad."

"Sure, not a problem." Fraser smiled up from his patient chart at the nurse. She was clearly well past smitten and deep in the throes of love. He knew the feeling. At least, from a noncommittal point of view. In the few moments of hard-core honesty he afforded himself, he'd lost count of the number of times he could've happily thrown caution to the wind, swept Tara up in his arms and kissed her with a hunger he'd not imagined possible.

Between the clinic, a few gratefully received general surgery shifts down at the Valley Hospital and a handful of snowboarding lessons from one of the local hotshots, he'd been run off his feet.

The past few weeks had been a revelation. For

the first time in the last four years he had felt peaceful. That night at the Blue…holding Tara in his arms, swaying to the music…had felt natural, real. Even laughing themselves silly at Fraser's attempts at becoming a tenpin bowling king. He'd definitely fallen into the jester role that night.

Well, there was a first time for everything. And firsts were coming at him faster than snowflakes up here. After years of taking flight at the first sign of happiness, he could see why Tara wanted to put down roots and stay here in Deer Creek. The location was downright beautiful, there was a fun group of people here, living a surprisingly lively social scene despite the waxing and waning seasonal population. They were good folk and it was easy to understand how she had found such comfort in the straightforward nature of the locals. They were loyal. Kind. They were stayers.

Dropping Tara off last night after the gondola ride back up from the Valley had been a genuine test of his mettle. He'd tossed a cavalier "See ya" out into the night when all he'd really wanted to do had been to scoop her up in his arms, carry her up those rickety steps of hers and make mind-blowing love to her. Not to mention letting her know where she stood with the Valley Hospital. But that wasn't on the cards. All *that* sang of commitment and was still a big no-go area.

Fraser popped the finished chart into the filing pile and stared at the front door of the clinic, willing someone to come in. As long as he kept busy, everything would be fine.

Who was he kidding? Nothing was going to keep him busy enough to keep his thoughts away from Tara for long. Like right now. He cocked his head to the side and closed his eyes, fine-tuned to the gentle creaking of the floorboards above his head. It meant she was back from her ER shift in the valley. X-ray glasses wouldn't go amiss right about now. Images of Tara standing in her kitchen in that fluffy red towel of hers flitted past his closed lids. It was a bit too easy to imagine it falling to the floor. He rubbed his fingers across his eyes, willing the provocative imaginings away. Too distracting.

Pushing back from the desk, Fraser headed to the office computer in the next room with the intention of looking up obscure skiing injuries online. It was never a bad time to swot up. Especially with Tara as a colleague. She was an exceptionally good doctor and never took the easiest path if another course of action was going to benefit the patient in the long run.

He heard the radio crackling to life on Liesel's desk. Good. He jogged into the main room to listen with her. Something to do.

"This is Ski Patrol Three. Deer Creek Clinic, can you read me? Over."

Liesel picked up the transmitter and confirmed the signal.

"Gear up. There's been an avalanche on the Shadow Peak Pass. We need all hands on deck. Over."

"Where's Eric?" Liesel abandoned radio protocol, her face draining of blood.

"Chopper will be ready for the docs in two minutes, Liesel. You'd best stay and man the clinic."

Panic flooded the redhead's green eyes, her face blanched in fear. Fraser automatically reached out a reassuring hand to squeeze her shoulder, certain it would be of little comfort. He knew as well as she did what the ski patroller on the other end of the line was saying.

Eric was involved in the avalanche. They didn't know where he was.

* * *

Tara ran into the clinic through the back door, radio in one hand, bright red ski jacket in the other. Standard issue for on-site rescue crews. Protocol was essential right now.

"Liesel, you can do this." She held the nurse by her shoulders, mustering up the most reassuring smile she could. Sure, it was a grim smile, but working without hope wasn't an option.

Behind her, Tara was aware of Fraser raiding the supply cabinet to load their emergency medical backpacks and totes, but for the next few seconds she needed to focus on her friend. "We've got to slow your breathing down, Liesel." Tara knew hyperventilation in times of stress was a possibility and losing the nurse to a panic attack was the last thing they needed. "We're going to go out and find him, okay?"

Even as she made the promise, she knew it wasn't hers to make. The mountains could be dangerous. At least a dozen snowboarders and skiers lost their lives across the Rockies every year and sometimes even the utmost precaution was no help in the face of a mountain covered in hazards.

Liesel clutched at Tara, her fingernails making painful half-moon impressions into the backs of her hands. The scratches were nothing compared to the pain she could only imagine, Liesel was feeling as she pleaded, "I want to go. Please let me come with you."

"No. You're too close to this. You've got to stay at the clinic, man the radio, take care of anyone who comes in. We'll get a medic to come up from the Valley, but you're in charge now, okay?"

Tears began to flow freely from her friend's eyes. It broke Tara's heart, knowing there was nothing she could do to stem the flow. "Look, Eric's experienced at this. He's always got his beacons on, and everyone on the mountain will help with the search, not just the ski patrol." Liesel swiped at her tears, unable to speak. Tara pulled her petite friend into a close hug, suddenly concerned she'd been wrong to press her to work. "C'mon. We're going to set you up at Marian's. We can bring the radios and everything there. We'll put a sign up for patients to come to the bakery."

"No. I'm going to stay here." Liesel grounded herself, her tone adamant.

"Really, Li—you don't have to."

"Yes, I do. Eric would be furious if he found out I'd abandoned the clinic."

She didn't blame Liesel for wanting to go to the site. She would do the same if someone she loved were in danger. *If Fraser were in danger.*

An icy chill shot through her. Not something she could consider. Not with how she was beginning to feel about him. How she did feel about him? Already something told her wolves couldn't have stopped her from being out there, digging with everyone else, if he was in danger.

She shook the thoughts away. Right now there wasn't time for speculating. She had to trust Liesel's professional skills and get out onto the mountain. Avalanche victims had an hour, maximum, if they were unable to find a pocket of air to breathe. Crews would already be out searching for victims, but the more people who were on hand to help, the better.

"Ready?"

"Mmm…" Tara wished Fraser knew how much his voice was like a soothing tonic to her. He sounded the picture of calm. Another story ran through his eyes when she turned around to take her rescue backpack from him. Those normally deep blue eyes were black with—what was it, fear? Her mind sped through everything she knew about him. Very little. Whatever it was he hadn't told her, she could see this was going to be tough for him.

If she'd been able keep him here with Liesel, protect him from whatever it was he was dreading, she would. But lives were at stake and they needed him up on the peak.

The last thing in the world Fraser felt was calm. He hadn't been in a chopper since…well, since that day in Afghanistan. He was going to have to use every last ounce of his military training to keep his nerves in check. There were at least a dozen lives on the line up there and he was one of a small team who'd have to save them. No failure. Not this time.

He'd had avalanche training in the forces but hadn't needed to put it to use. Rescuing people was hard enough, but having to do it in unstable conditions with limited visibility increased the stakes for the victims. Time was of the essence.

He watched Tara as she jogged out onto the

helipad to join him. Seeing her beautiful face, a picture of concentration and professional focus, helped shore up his reserves. He could do this. He needed to do this. The past was exactly where it was—there was nothing he could do to change it now. It was time to live in the moment.

Time took on an otherworldly quality as he felt the helicopter lift from the ground, tenuously at first, then in rapid flight up towards the pass. A bitter taste rose in his throat. The familiar physical sensations, the sounds of the helicopter blades whirring into high speed, they were all acute reminders of the last time he'd flown. Fraser had left base camp that morning with a brother and returned home without one. All in the space of an hour. He flinched away the similarities of the situation. No time to dwell on them. Each second was precious now. Within an hour they would know if anyone had survived. He suddenly felt fingers reaching across his hand. Giving it a reassuring squeeze. *Tara.*

Her eyes were squarely focused on the helicopter's trajectory but she seemed to have a second sense that he needed something—reassurance.

Balance. Her small gesture meant more to him than she would ever know.

No, he didn't have his brother any more, but at least he had Tara. For now.

In no time at all they had soared across to the western side of the peaks and one of the heli-rescue team was gesturing to Fraser that it was time to clip on his belaying equipment.

"We don't think the ground is stable enough to land." The pilot's voice crackled through his headset. Fraser gave a thumbs-up to the two-strong heli-rescue team who had accompanied them. Until a safe landing was established they would have to go down to the site by rope, carrying the stretchers and medical kits with them.

"Do we know how many victims are down there?"

The sound of Tara's voice through the headset was like a life-affirming elixir to him, despite the fact her words were strictly limited to the rescue mission.

"Negative. We think about five, but the crew on the ground should know more. Snowboarders," finished the pilot, as if that answered everything.

Fraser felt his lips curve into a grimace. Snowboarders were seen as the wild cards on the slopes. Willing to take more risks, push beyond the prescribed limits. He could hardly cast aspersions. He'd nearly taken Tara out the first day he'd met her, taking such a risk. Even idiots deserved a second chance. Even idiots like him.

Below him, Fraser could see three snowmobiles and about half a dozen ski patrollers armed with probes, fanning out across the small bowl of mountainside that curved along the west side of the pass. Not having time to register the two-hundred-meter drop he was about to make, Fraser double-checked that his harnesses and sling were securely fastened. He could see Tara giving her harness straps the final snug tugs into place and had to restrain himself from reaching over and double-checking all her gear as well. If there was one person he wanted to keep safe… Well, she was right there beside him, preparing to jump out of a helicopter onto an unstable mountain pass.

"See you down there." Tara pushed her feet away from the edge of the helicopter and disappeared from his sight. *Yes, you will.*

Tara's adrenaline was running high. She'd only made a helicopter drop a couple of times and with so many factors to consider for the rescue she found herself having to take her own advice to Liesel. Even, slow breaths. Panic was the last thing she needed to be showing now.

"We've got one over here!"

Barely having time to register the scene as a whole, Tara set off in the direction of a patroller waving a red flag at her. Progress had to be slow, steady, to avoid collapsing into the snow. Her energy re-formed into a focused charge of motivation. Get to the victims. Taking the path the patrollers indicated, Tara made her way as quickly as possible through the soft snow, stretcher in tow, to the figure they were digging out. So far only a pair of booted feet were visible. Tara could hardly comprehend how the crashing wall of snow had flipped the snowboarder entirely upside down.

"Soft-slab avalanche." The patroller spoke in the staccato of someone limiting themselves to facts only. "Looks to be about twenty yards wide and four, maybe five feet deep."

"What do you want me to do?" Facts and actions. Tara knew those were the only two options available to her right now.

"Can you help me dig around him? Until we know if he has any neck injuries, we shouldn't move him." The ski patroller handed her a collapsible shovel. Right now, rescue efforts would be confined to getting air to the victims. As long as their heads were buried, the chances of suffocation increased by the second.

"Have they found Eric?"

Tara kept her voice low, hoping it would mask the emotion she felt.

"Not sure, Doc." The blond patroller, who she was pretty sure was called Chris, answered. He abruptly dropped his shovel and began to dig with his hands as they reached what they could now see was a young man's face, his eyes blinking in the bright sunshine.

"I'm Dr. Braxton. You're safe now. Can you tell me what you're feeling?"

Through chattering teeth he replied, "My shoulder. My shoulder is killing me."

Tara gently released the man's fingers from the snow pack. "Can you feel my hand?"

"A little." She exhaled a sigh of relief. As long as he had sensation they were all right. "It's

Chris, right?" she looked at the patroller, who nodded a brisk affirmation.

"Chris, can we get—? What's your name?" She looked into the young man's hazel eyes.

"Brian."

"Can we get Brian flat out on the snow pack? I can do a quick assessment and you can move on."

"Got it, Doc."

After gently moving the young man to a horizontal position, stretched out on one of Tara's emergency body-heat blankets, she quickly assessed he'd dislocated his shoulder.

"Have they found everyone else?" Brian's voice wasn't much more than a whisper.

"The crews are doing the best they can." Tara offered a smile to the young man, who was clearly scared out of his wits.

"We thought we'd try the new powder."

"It's a big temptation." Tara tried to keep her voice level. Untouched snow, unexplored gullies on the far side of the mountain, they were all lures to adrenaline junkies. They could be as thrilling as they were dangerous. Today it was just plain dangerous.

"This is going to hurt, Brian. We'll get you

something for the pain later, but for now can you just bite onto this?" Tara put a thick roll of gauze between his teeth. Bracing herself as best she could against the soft-packed snow, Tara pulled his shoulder back into position. With a quick signal to the heli-crew, Tara received additional help moving Brian onto a stretcher and getting him loaded aboard the hovering helicopter.

A few yards away she saw Fraser attending to a young woman. Judging from the red snow around her, she had suffered some fairly serious cuts. Lacerations were difficult to avoid in an avalanche filled with pieces of rock and other debris. If the cuts were all she'd suffered, she was lucky. If they became infected, the likelihood of a hospital stay increased.

Calls came out across the rescue site at a rapid rate of knots. One, two, three, four of the snowboarders were found. One had a broken leg, one had a pretty severe eye injury. Still no Eric.

Tara's adrenaline surged through her. She had to help the crews find him. Spying Chris probing the snow near a small cluster of trees, she shouldered her medical pack and worked her way carefully towards him. Avalanches easily destabilized the snow table. Disturbing it further always posed a risk of more trouble. All things considered, this had been a relatively small soft-slab avalanche set off by foot penetration. Snowboarders and skiers didn't normally start these. She scanned the scene, looking for equipment, but everything was a wash of white, accented only by the rescue team in their bright red ski jackets.

Someone must've taken off their snowboard at the top of the peak and walked for a bit, or maybe adjusted a boot heavily—she didn't know. Whatever it was, it didn't matter now. A terrifying course of events had been set in motion and now it was up to the team here to fight against time and find everyone swept under the potentially lethal snow shelf.

"How wide was the slide?"

Tara's sensory awareness kicked up another notch, hearing Fraser's soft burr beside her.

"The team reckons it was about fifteen meters wide—and only about a meter or so deep, which is why they were able to get everyone out so quickly..."

She stopped, all too aware they hadn't found everyone yet. Eric and a snowboarder named

Katie were still unaccounted for. Time seemed to have stood still, but only fifteen or twenty minutes had passed. Crucial minutes.

"I've got a beacon!" Chris's voice cut through the sharp mountain air. Tara felt her heart soar. All the ski medics wore them. She turned to Fraser and had to restrain herself from throwing her arms around him. "Eric!"

Fraser's broad grin matched her own. He gave her gloved hand a quick squeeze then began to make his way carefully to the site Chris had indicated. The positive surge of energy she received from the contact with Fraser gave her the added boost she needed. The work, combined with the altitude, was exhausting. Never mind the ten-hour shift she'd just finished in the ER down in the Valley. Her own fatigue could not factor on her radar now. Liesel would want news, and soon. She'd call straight away, unless—

Don't even go there, Tara. Not yet, anyway.

Giving her hands a quick shake for warmth, Tara took her collapsible shovel and began to pull away the soft top layer of snow as quickly as she could to make a safe path.

"Watch yourselves," Chris cautioned, his face

the picture of concentration as he shoveled away at the icy snow. "This is a pretty deep tree well."

"Where do you want us?" Fraser looked the picture of a military man, waiting for orders, ready for action. Tara felt a swell of pride pass through her chest. Whatever mental hurdles he had been trying to overcome as they'd left base, he had cleared them in spades. If it were possible for the professional esteem she had for him to increase, now was the moment.

"The beacon's right here." Chris pointed to a spot a couple of feet from the large pine tree.

The three worked silently, shoveling the snow away diligently from the light glowing dimly through the snow. First they revealed Eric's booted feet, then his legs. The snow must have swept him head first into the tree well. Seconds felt like minutes as Tara prayed he'd had time to deploy his Avalung, an invaluable device all the ski patrollers wore as standard issue. They allowed anyone caught in an avalanche to breathe for up to an hour—but, crucially, only if they were able to get the mouthpiece in place before the snow swept over them.

Please, let Eric have been so lucky.

The sub-zero air bit at Tara's face, the odd shard of icy snow stinging her cheeks, but she didn't care. This was the first avalanche rescue she'd worked on and the power of the mountain overwhelmed her. One moment five snowboarders had been out having a great time, and the next?

She felt her fingers press against something firm. Abandoning her shovel, she began to tear at the snow, revealing the tell-tale red fabric of a ski patroller's jacket. A quick exchange of glances and Chris and Fraser formed an even tighter circle round the beacon, clearing the snow away as quickly as they could, but with the highest level of care. If Eric had sustained a neck injury, any sort of quick movement or a further collapse of the soft snow shelf could paralyze him permanently. Or worse.

"Eric? Can you hear me, mate?" Fraser repeated the question again and again as he exposed the patroller's face. There was no sign that he'd been using the Avalung and repeated attempts to elicit a response from him proved fruitless. Eric's skin was icy cold, his head twisted, almost compressed into his right shoulder. Tara's stomach constricted. As if in a trance, she watched Fraser pull off a glove and press two fingers against Eric's neck, looking up at Tara as he did so. "Weak pulse."

She heaved a sigh of relief. At least he was alive.

"Let's get him out and onto a stretcher. It'll be a couple of minutes before the helicopter is back." Chris's voice was grim. This was his friend and it was easy to see he was struggling to keep control of his emotions.

Chris had already waved the red flag and the members of the ski patrol who weren't looking for the missing young woman hurried over with a stretcher. After putting a neck brace around Chris's neck, the team carefully moved him onto the bright yellow stretcher and wrapped him in heat blankets.

"You'd better go with him." Fraser's voice was grave after returning his fingers to Eric's pulse point.

Tara felt her eyes snap to his. Normally the heli-rescue team handled the people they were sending up.

"Just go." Raw emotion ripped across his eyes

in an appeal to her to consent to his request. What was going through his head? What had hurt him so deeply?

"Come with me."

Tara knew it was a risk, but she had faith it was one worth taking. Something told her Fraser needed her now, and something deep within her was saying they should stay together.

"We're losing him." Jagged shards of emotion tore at Fraser's throat as he spoke the words.

Tara pressed her fingers to Eric's pulse point. Nothing.

"We need to apply CPR." Training took over as she flew into action, beginning the familiar movements of cardiopulmonary resuscitation. As she pressed her hands together and began to perform the syncopated rhythms to revive Eric's heart, she locked eyes with Fraser. He needed to be on-point if this was going to work.

"We need help over here!"

The call came from the ski patrollers working on the young woman they had finally managed to dig out.

"You go." She tipped her head in the direction of the other crew.

Fraser knew Tara was offering him a lifeline. In an instant she had read the scenario for what it was. This was the first time he'd had to care for someone he knew and, more importantly, cared about since he'd lost his brother. Up until now, caring had been a very, very big no-go zone for him. Eric, like his brother, was a young man in love with an incredible future ahead of him. He'd confessed to Fraser, over a game of pool, that he was planning on asking Liesel to marry him.

At the time Fraser had envied Eric's assured understanding of what he wanted—love, marriage and a life up in Deer Creek, doing what he loved best. Fraser knew in his soul he wanted those things, too, but Eric was ready to act on them. His confidence in life, in living, was infectious. Eric and Liesel would make a great couple. He looked at Tara, certain now of what he had to do.

How could he let Eric go now just because he was having a "moment"?

"I've got this one."

Tara looked up from her hands, still offering

regular compressions to Eric's chest. Her dark eyes spoke volumes.

"You sure?"

"I've got it. Go to the other patient—it's a bone break. That's more your turf than mine."

Tara hesitated.

"Go." Fraser felt the turbulence of indecision clear away. Medical training took precedence over emotion. He was going to do everything in his power to get Eric back to Valley Hospital alive.

CHAPTER NINE

"So, WHAT YOU'RE telling me is you're going to try to turn her cartilage into bone?" Katie's father looked at Tara incredulously before taking a protective glance into his daughter's hospital room.

"It's her best chance of seeing that collarbone really heal, Mr. Fremont. We can put pins in, but there are risks. The clavicle lies above some crucial nerves and blood vessels. If the bones shift at all during healing, Katie could face significant risks. Plates and screws are standard and will help her, but I believe the risks associated with the hardware left inside Katie after surgery could be eliminated by trying this new method."

"But your techniques are experimental."

It was impossible to miss the worry in the Fremonts' eyes and Tara could hardly blame them. Yes, the technique was experimental. But it was also one she had the most confidence in. She knew the methodology of this operation better than anyone. After a brief exploratory surgery she'd known instinctively the young woman was a perfect candidate for the trial. It would be a risk, but one she fervently believed would be in the patient's best interests.

Heart in mouth, she had asked to speak to the head of the hospital. Incredibly, the hospital chair had known about her research since her arrival in Deer Valley. As soon as the news of her ex's failure to move her research forward had broken, he'd been working with the medical council to transfer the intellectual rights. Tara could hardly believe her ears as she heard him tell her they'd hoped for a long time that they could lure her into working on the technique at the hospital. Now, not ten minutes after taking what she thought was a massive risk, she was enjoying the full support of the hospital with a promise to discuss future research when they had more time. Euphoric or not—flying high on her own success was not what was important now. Katie and her parents deserved the freedom to choose.

"It is just one opinion, but I think this would be your best chance for good healing, Mr. and Mrs. Fremont."

She watched the couple share a look—one heavy with mutual trust and love—and couldn't help feeling a twinge of envy. She let herself wonder for an instant how Fraser was doing.

She had heard through the heli-team that he was in surgery with Eric. It was a good sign. It meant Eric was still alive.

"Cartilage is incredibly robust." Tara felt a burst of passion charge through her as she refocused. This was her area of expertise and it never failed to fire her enthusiasm. Despite the politics of medical research, she had always enjoyed the actual work. Discovering the body's physical and biochemical ability to communicate with the skeleton had been a real window into understanding how cells could be "told" to become cartilage or bone cells. Right now, Katie needed bone cells and Tara, with the permission of her parents, knew she could help set their daughter's body on a corrective healing path. If only they would give their consent.

Again, she watched as the couple bent their heads together, silently trying to come to some sort of decision. That sort of quiet communication only came with years of shared history.

Years she now ached to share with someone. No. That wasn't right. Not just anyone. A very particular Scottish someone.

"You don't have to decide this minute." Tara laid a hand on Mrs. Fremont's shoulder. "It's a big decision. Why don't you take a break, go and get some coffee and we'll meet up once you've had a chance to digest everything. If there's anything you want to know, anything at all, just page me."

The couple smiled gratefully and headed off to the canteen. Tara felt herself tugged towards the surgical ward. She wanted an update on Eric and, she couldn't help admitting, she wanted an update on Fraser.

He'd shown incredible fortitude up on the mountain, his medical skills overriding any personal trauma he might have been experiencing. Not many people were able face their fears head on. She didn't feel so much surprised by the revelation as comforted. He was a man she would want to be with in a crisis. If only he wanted to stay here in Deer Creek, give settling down a chance.

She felt her teeth begin the familiar pinch along her lower lip. She'd come to know Fraser pretty well over the past few weeks. It was clear they shared a mutual attraction. Playing it slow had been hard. For both of them. It didn't take a Nobel prizewinner to notice they each had to actively restrain themselves from sharing any more of those incredible kisses. Kisses she re-lived each time she closed her eyes at night. And slow dances for that matter.

Tara renewed her quick pace to try and shake the images away. Not easy. A spiral of warmth gently ribboned up her spine, sending tingles of electricity along her neck and scalp. She pulled her hands through her hair, trying to scrub away the sensation as she approached the surgical ward. Dreaming of more time with Fraser be-yond the ski season was useless. If there was one thing she was sure about, commitment was not his game.

"He's clotting." Fraser's voice was tight as he set the surgical staff back in motion. An arterial embolism or blood clot was the last thing Eric needed. They had only just managed to keep his heart pumping throughout the helicopter trip to Valley Hospital. Whether or not he had sustained any brain damage was yet to be determined, but a blocked artery could spell immediate death.

Fraser felt as if he was watching himself go through the motions. He knew them well. Working as a trauma surgeon in the military, he had been through this operation a hundred, no, countless times. Some made it, some didn't.

"He's stroking." The nurse spoke the words out loud, although everyone in the room could see it happening.

They worked silently, diligently. The chances of Eric living a normal life had already passed. As the moments slipped past Fraser knew in his heart what the rest of the staff had already taken on board. They were losing him. They were losing Eric and the only person unwilling to see the situation for what it was was himself.

"Just stay with me." He doubted the staff could've heard the plea he'd whispered behind his surgical mask. He felt himself going into overdrive, unable to bear losing Eric. Sure, they were new friends, had only known each other a handful of weeks, but the young man's faith in life, his unshakeable belief in the value of taking the risk of love and marriage—committing to someone for life—had really struck him.

For Fraser, falling in love with Tara was a forbidden pleasure. Staying in Deer Creek, seeing her through life's ups and downs? He ached for it, but fought against his belief that he didn't deserve to enjoy that level of happiness. Watching Eric make decisions about his life and his relationship with Liesel had helped Fraser feel less lost at sea as he tried to come to terms with healing his own wounds from the past. If an adrenaline junkie like Eric could settle down, there was certainly hope for him. Wasn't there?

The tell-tale tone from the heart monitor brought the situation to a head. After two hours of surgery Eric had flatlined. They had exhausted all their options. A dozen pairs of eyes in the OR turned to him, waiting for instructions.

Unable to say the words himself, Eric nodded at one of the Valley Hospital general surgeons. "Call it."

"Time of death: four-forty-five p.m."

As his surgical team closed up procedures on Eric, watching Fraser pull off his gown and leave the room tore at Tara's heart. Numbness crept into her limbs as she began to register what had happened.

Eric was dead.

She couldn't even begin to fathom how Liesel was going to take the news, let alone his family. Instinct took over. She left the observation booth intent on finding Fraser. Losing Eric would be a terrible blow to him. Not just because losing any patient was painful but also because she'd seen a friendship developing between the two men over the past few weeks. A friendship that had given her the occasional flicker of hope that Fraser might just consider staying.

She looked everywhere. No Fraser. It was as if he'd vanished into thin air. Despite her best efforts, Tara felt the beginnings of a small fissure of panic working its way into her psyche. *Please, let him stay.*

After what seemed like hours, but had probably been less than one, Tara finally spied the familiar thatch of chestnut hair. Still dressed in his scrubs, Tara watched as Fraser slowly sank into a chair, head cradled in his hands. Raw emotion burned her throat, choking away the words of comfort she had hoped to share with him. Tears stung her eyes as she approached him. His stillness was so complete it seemed to create an invisible barrier between them.

She ached to help him. He wouldn't go through this alone, not if she could help it. Tara felt herself reach out and run her fingers through his hair, a gesture her mother used to do to her when she was sad. With Fraser, it felt incredibly intimate. As she repeated the gesture, she felt him gently lean his head so that some of its weight rested in her hand, a small groan escaping his lips. Never before had she felt such pain in witnessing someone else's sorrow.

"I'm so sorry, Fraser. I saw the surgery and there was nothing you could have done."

Lifting his face from his hands, Fraser's expression was a transparent exposé of the agony he was feeling. Tears clouded his eyes as he wordlessly pulled her towards him, a hand drawing across her thighs so that she came to a seated position on his lap. His scent flooded her senses to the extent she felt he was physically a part of her. Fraser wordlessly buried his head in the crook of her shoulder as if trying to find a way to hide from everything he was feeling.

Suddenly, abruptly, Fraser wrapped his arms around her, pulling her closer into him as if holding her was the only thing in the world he could do right now. Tearless sobs shuddered through him. His arms pulled her in even tighter with a fierceness she hadn't known before. Somehow, through his grief, Fraser was including her, silently inviting her to share their sorrow together. The gesture felt selfless, inclusive. Tears flooded her eyes as the full weight of the day's events began to make its lasting impression.

As doctors, they saw death more than most, but it never made it easier. Cases like this, involving loved ones—how could you not feel anguish? No doubt Fraser's sorrow bore the additional burden of his hidden grief. She hoped with all her heart he could share it with her someday—lighten the load. The drive to save Eric that she had seen in him spoke to her. Spoke to her of a man who would stop at nothing if it meant saving a life. She hadn't believed the intensity of emotion she felt growing within her for Fraser the past few weeks could have deepened.

Would a future without this man be possible? Would she be able to open her heart up that freely again? Not that he'd offered it as an option. But here in the hospital corridor, the hustle and bustle of the hospital blurring into white noise, arms wrapped around each other, it was as if nothing else mattered.

Fraser must have heard Tara's name over the Tannoy system first.

"Sounds like you're needed, Dr. Braxton." He cleared his throat and flicked his eyes up towards the speaker above them.

She felt his arms release her, his hands slip slowly down her arms as if reluctant to let go. She knew how he felt.

"It must be the Fremonts. They'll have made a decision about Katie's surgery, I expect." Tara stood up, taking a quick scan of the hallway for a bathroom. She definitely needed to splash some cold water on her face before facing Katie's parents.

"Ah, yes." He raked a hand through his hair before raising a mysterious brow in her direction. "How could I forget?"

Tara watched as Fraser's eyes darkened. Strange. He couldn't know anything about Katie's surgery.

"I've got to get back to the Fremonts."

Fraser stretched his arms up to the ceiling before folding them in what seemed like a solid closed-for-Business gesture across his chest.

"Go. I'm fine." His voice was flat. Tara's heart felt as though it was going through a shredder. She longed to hold him again, be held by him and share their collective grief. Yet her professional ethics were paramount and she wouldn't keep the Fremonts waiting. Particularly now that she might have a chance to use her new procedure.

"I'll probably be a while. See you back in Deer Creek?"

Fraser could hear the hopefulness in her voice. He wanted to respond to it, knew he must respond to it, but felt as though his body had been taken over by some sort of speech paralysis.

He offered her a nod and a half-wave, a feeble attempt to convey the tidal wave of emotion he was experiencing.

Watching her retreat down the hall, Fraser felt a

physical ache of loss. Eric didn't have the chance he had now. If he didn't take it, let Tara know how she had upended his world in the best way possible, he knew he'd win the prize for international idiot of the year. His brother would've handed him the ribbon himself. If he'd been there.

He punched at the empty corridor, willing it to take him on. Something was going to have to change. Holding her, Fraser had felt as though Tara and he had become a single unit. One incredibly strong, able, fearless person who could take on life's disappointments and grow stronger. And yet none of that diminished the fact that she was an extraordinary individual. He didn't want to change a single thing about her. He hadn't missed the glint of excitement crackling in her eyes as she'd mentioned her procedure. A spark of passion he hadn't felt for a while. Hadn't *allowed* himself to feel. He'd been too heavy with guilt, with grief, and had allowed them to darken his world rather than appreciate everything he did have.

"Tara." He heard her name escape his lips then gave a dry laugh. His utterance had sounded a little close to Scarlett O'Hara's final cry at the end of *Gone With the Wind* as she'd mourned her beloved plantation, now burnt to the ground. What to do now?

He turned towards the hospital exit with an explosion of purpose he hadn't anticipated. At last. He knew exactly what to do.

Tara stared at the Fremonts, unable to believe what she was hearing.

"I'm sorry. Who was it who convinced you we should go ahead with the surgery?"

The Fremonts glanced at each other before explaining again. "We were in the canteen when a Scottish doctor came in. He overheard us weighing up our options at the coffee bar and—"

Mrs. Fremont quickly interrupted her husband's story. "He wasn't being rude—we were standing side by side."

"No, that's right. He was very polite. Anyhow, Dr. MacKenzie, I believe he said his name was, told us we couldn't be in safer hands. He seemed very aware of the surgery and assured us you would only do what was best for Katie."

Tara sat back in shock as she digested what the Fremonts were saying. Directly after Eric's surgery—after Fraser had lost a patient—his first action had been to champion her. It was one of the most selfless things she had ever heard. Would she ever fully understand this man? Offering the Fremonts a relieved smile, her heart full of gratitude, she stood and gestured in the direction of Katie's room. "Shall we have a chat with your daughter?"

Tara screamed as the thick pair of mittens closed over her eyes. She whirled around as fast as she could then lost her footing on the snowy front porch of the clinic and slipped to the ground. In a desperate attempt to get away she began to scrabble on her hands and knees away from the large pair of strangely familiar boots following her.

"Tara, it's me!"

Relief flooded through her at the sound of the chocolaty rich voice. "What are you doing here?" She sat back, leaning against the clinic wall to catch her breath as she took in the sight of a mortified-looking Fraser.

"I'm so sorry!"

Nervous laughter burbled out of Tara's lips as she accepted Fraser's extended hand to help her up. Still warm and reassuring. Still the one hand in the universe that turned her insides into an untamed flight of tummy flutters.

"You scared the daylights out of me!" Tara looked around the porch as if searching for answers to her questions. "I thought you'd gone back to your chalet."

Fraser picked up her handbag she'd dropped on the porch floor. "Apologies, apologies! Bad idea. It looks as though we are in danger of becoming the pratfall couple."

Tara knew it was only a throw-away comment, but Fraser mentioning them as a couple put her already jangled nerves into a right old tailspin. A life with Fraser? That'd be the day.

"Why don't you give me the keys to the clinic so I can lock up, and then let's get you a glass of wine," he continued, completely unaware of the fact Tara already had herself walking down the aisle straight into his unsuspecting arms. She handed him the keys, happy to catch a glimpse of the smile she'd been hoping to see since they parted ways at the hospital. The last twenty-four hours had been exhausting. Between the hospital, the clinic, losing Eric, informing Liesel, not to mention Eric's family…

Tara allowed herself a moment to lean against the doorframe, just soaking in the quiet mountain ambience. She turned her head. The mountains weren't the only nice thing to look at around here. A smile teased at her lips as she drank in Fraser's profile, all sexy angles, dark hair and long-lashed eyes. *Oh, Lordy. There goes the strength in my knees again.*

Wine? Fraser? A dangerous combination. Particularly when it seemed she owed him untold thanks for tipping the Fremont's decision-making process in her direction.

Fraser handed back her keys and took one of her hands in his. *Thanks, Fraser, more delectable tummy flutters!*

"This was meant to be a surprise, but perhaps going into things eyes wide open might be a good idea."

"Why are you talking in riddles?"

He tipped his head in the direction of Main Street. "C'mon. You'll see."

Tara followed wordlessly as Fraser led her along

the recently cleared path towards what should have been a closed Marian's Bakery.

Was that candlelight she saw on her favorite mountain-view table?

As if in a dream, she passed through the bakery door Fraser held open for her. A sharp intake of breath was the only response she could muster as she took in the shop's transformation.

Artfully rolled beeswax candles burned with a warm luster on her favorite table—a Formica 1950s affair now hidden beneath a thick, white linen tablecloth. Tiny fairy-lights twinkled around the window's edges, having been woven around the curtain rail. The well-lit windows of the lodge glowed warmly in the distance.

Poinsettias, red and white, decorated the small bar where customers normally stood to enjoy a quick croissant or hot chocolate before hitting the slopes for another couple of well-fortified hours. Her fingers flew to her mouth to stem a laugh of pure joy when she saw an artful arrangement of turkey-shaped gingerbread cookies presented as a centerpiece on the table. The aromas of a hot meal floated through the air. The scents of turkey and gravy were wafting around the store. Out of the corner of her eye she spied a couple of pies on a nearby table.

If anyone had asked her to describe how she felt at that moment, Tara would have had to confess she felt completely and utterly filled with joy. This was what she had imagined being in love was like. Never before had anyone gone to this sort of effort for her. Was this what it was like to be courted? Her ex had never even bothered and she had been so naïve at the time it hadn't occurred to her that business dinners weren't meant to double as dates.

Running a single finger along the counter, Tara allowed herself to walk into the center of the bakery and take a slow turn, almost frightened that if she moved too quickly she would discover the whole scene had been a figment of her imagination.

Who was she kidding? The last few weeks had been a dream. A fairly turbulent dream to be sure, but from the moment Fraser MacKenzie had walked, no, snowboarded into her world, it had been as if life in Deer Creek had turned into one of those magic snow globes she'd had as a child.

"I know the real one didn't measure up to

much, so I thought we could have another stab at it. Happy Thanksgiving, Tara."

She felt Fraser's presence before that incredible Scottish brogue of his shivered its way down her spine.

Unable to turn and face him, Tara found herself fanning away the emotion threatening to escape her eyes. "I-I don't know what to s-say." She stammered to a halt, her voice barely a whisper.

Gently turning her round to face him, Fraser held Tara at arm's length, a broad smile working its way across his lips. One look at her face told him the answer to everything he'd been wondering for the last few hours. The effort had been worth it. Not bad for a fellow who'd never had a Thanksgiving in his life.

Tears shone in those perfectly rich brown eyes of hers, glinting off her wet lashes as if willing him to lean down and kiss them away. He hardly believed it was possible, but seeing Tara in the soft candlelight brought out an even greater beauty in her. Her white-as-milk skin was like a smooth invitation to reach out and stroke her cheek, to run a finger along her feminine jawline towards those plump, cherry lips.

It was all but impossible to keep his hands to himself. But keep himself in check was exactly what he was going to do. This was phase one of his new take on life. He'd asked Tara for a future of friendship. His gut had been telling him he wanted more, would never be satisfied solely with friendship. It was, however, the foundation of some of the best relationships he had ever seen. So…

Take it slow, MacKenzie.

If the military had taught him anything, it was discipline. Fraser heard his gut, his brain, hell, every particle in his body putting out a red alert, telling him he wanted Tara Braxton in his life for good. If he was going to win this woman, win her and keep her, he would have to make sure he didn't frighten her away. And he would have to make sure he could deliver on everything he already wanted to promise her. Any hint of emotional intimacy over the past four years had sent him straight to the airport. Not that there had been anyone who'd come this close to setting his heart aflame. And right now it was on fire.

Adopting the formal tone of a hoity-toity French waiter, Fraser motioned towards the table he'd laid out. "Mademoiselle, I believe your dinner awaits."

Tara accepted the arm Fraser offered even though the distance they had to cover couldn't have been more than six or seven steps. Her fingertips tingled as she slipped them into the crook of his arm, once again close enough to breathe in his mountain-scented maleness. It was all she could do not to press her cheek against his chest and inhale.

Calm, Tara. Keep calm.

Sliding into her chair, Tara couldn't help letting out another laugh of pleasure as she took in even more seasonal knick-knacks Fraser had apparently spirited out of thin air. Crêpe paper turkeys, pumpkin-motif napkins, miniature pilgrim hats nestled below the candle stands. "Where on earth did you get all this? I feel as if I'm Dorothy and have landed in a North Pole version of Oz!"

She watched as those strong, capable-looking hands of his poised above two silver-domed plates, her mind in a whirl of thoughts.

"Ahh," Fraser intoned, tapping the side of his nose mischievously. "That's for me to know and you to spend the rest of the season wondering. Although…" He leant back for a moment, fingers stroking his chin thoughtfully. "If you're in Oz does that make me the Wizard or Toto?"

"I know who you're not."

"Who's that then?" He leaned forward looking just about as gorgeous as she had ever seen him.

"The mayor or Lilliput."

She made a "sorry" face for her poor attempt at witty banter. It was all she could do to latch onto one thought at a time and process it. The last ten minutes had been nothing less than a collection of sensual teases. Come to think of it, his last statement had been on the coy side. What had he meant by "the season"? Was he just warning her all this was temporary? Tara felt herself bite down on her lip again, sharply this time, before daring to look into Fraser's eyes. Dangerously attractive eyes shining a bright, incredible midnight blue in the candlelight.

She swallowed hard. He seemed genuine enough, and his words could have been a casual slip of the tongue rather than betraying his deepest intentions. He'd only ever offered her friend-ship. Could she afford herself one night? One night of thinking her dreams had come true?

"Is Madamoiselle ready for her first course?"

"Only," Tara intoned gravely, making her deci-sion, "if Monsieur has plans to join her."

"But of course!"

With a flourish Fraser lifted the silver domes to reveal two plates covered in aluminum foil. She saw a flash of dismay shoot across his face and couldn't help a fit of giggles from overwhelm-ing her.

He quickly pulled the foil away and revealed two plates laden with complete Thanksgiving dinners. There was the requisite turkey, a mound of stuffing, a tantalizing knob of butter cascad-ing down a snowy mountain of mashed potatoes, sweet potatoes complete with tiny marshmallows on top. A delicious-looking medley of peas, pearl onions and small bits of bacon rounded it all off.

"If Tara couldn't come to Thanksgiving," Fra-ser nodded in the direction of the lodge, "then Thanksgiving must come to Tara. Even if it is three weeks late."

Picking up her fork, Tara paused for a moment,

unable to resist reaching a hand across the small table to touch Fraser's as he sat down to join her. She had so much she wanted to thank him for but didn't trust herself to let loose the full force of gratitude she felt. Even so, the man deserved her thanks, however small. "Fraser MacKenzie, I don't know who you are, but this is just about one of the nicest things anyone has ever done for me."

"Surely not!" His tone was light, but she could tell he was touched by her words.

"I don't suppose you do this for all the ladies?" Tara could've kicked herself, practically seeing the words hang between them like an accusation. She saw a flash of—what was it?—sorrow cross Fraser's eyes at the mention of other women. *What was eating away at him?*

He stayed silent for a few moments, making busy work of rearranging his mashed potatoes.

Yup. She'd definitely put her foot in it. Tara felt her stomach churn with dismay. All this effort he'd gone to and her thoughtless comment had brought the mood crashing down. Why had she let her fears from the days of her ex dominate her life now? Those days were gone. Safely in the past. And here she was, dredging them up for everyone—well, Fraser—to see.

Fraser tilted his head up from his plate and answered soberly, "This night was supposed to be a thank-you for being there for me. That was it. But I suppose it's time I came clean."

Tara felt her throat constrict. What was he going to confess? That it was time to go? That their feverishly impassioned kisses had meant nothing? Surely not? *No, no, no!* She felt her fingers wrap round the edges of the chair seat as if trying to steel herself.

Avoiding her eyes, he continued, "You haven't really had a chance to get to truly know me yet. I doubt you'll be surprised to hear few people do. We're going to have to—" he stopped himself, clearly unhappy with his turn of phrase. He exhaled sharply, clearly frustrated with his inability to explain himself properly. "I don't think the Fraser MacKenzie you've met over the past few weeks has been a good example of the man I really am."

"I think I've seen a pretty good guy," Tara chanced. Sure, there had definitely been some rough-around-the-edges moments, but it was impossible not to see how kind and generous he was. How thoughtful. What she couldn't put a finger on was whatever Fraser was running away from, the horrible demons he seemed to be trying to escape.

He put down the wine bottle he'd been opening and rested his head in his hands for a moment. When he looked up his eyes betrayed a vulnerability that she had only caught fleeting glimpses of in the last few weeks. Glimpses that twisted her heart with compassion for him.

"No." He shook his head sadly. "That's just it, Tara. I am not a good guy." He took a ragged breath and unexpectedly the words began to flow. "Just over four years ago I was in Afghanistan with the British military, as you know. My brother was a lieutenant and I was a helicopter rescue pilot and field medic." He paused to take a deep draft of wine, as if fortifying himself for a long, difficult journey. Already his eyes had a faraway look. Tara couldn't help but feel incredibly moved. He was trusting her with a part of his history that was clearly painful to remember, let alone tell.

"Anyway, my brother was out on a mission one

day and I was at the base when we got a call. His squadron was under rebel attack. My team and I flew out as soon as we could. It quickly became clear Matt had placed himself between a couple of local families and the rebels in an effort to ward off their fire and save the families. Families largely comprised of women and children."

Tara caught herself holding her breath as Fraser's voice became more staccato, emotionless, as if he were delivering a military report. His face looked haunted, eyes weighted with grief. "We tried our best to create a safe zone where we could land, get the families out, get the team out, but there was too much heavy gunfire and someone from the rebel side came just a bit too close to the chopper with an RPG."

He shifted uncomfortably in his seat. It was all Tara could do not to slide her chair over to his side of the table and wrap her arms around him. Instinct told her he needed to continue, needed to tell her the whole story, so she stayed put.

"We finally managed to land safely and were able to load up about five women and all the children. Matt radioed in that we should take the families away, get them safe, while he and his squad would fall back to a location where we could pick them up later. He said they would be all right!" Fraser rasped, his eyes burning with emotion.

Tara reached her hands across the table to gently entwine her fingers with his. Her stomach was tied in knots, aching for the pain Fraser must have suffered, was still suffering.

"What happened next?" she asked.

"What do you think happened?" He pulled his hands away from hers sharply, his voice harsh. It wasn't personal. She knew that in her heart. Silently, Tara encouraged him to continue.

As if defeated, his shoulders slumped. Were it not for the quiet night, Tara doubted she would've heard him breathe out the words, "I was too late. Now his wife is a widow, with two beautiful children to raise all on her own. Children who will never know their father. All thanks to me. All this…" he waved an arm at the mountains looming outside the window "…the non-stop moving, the never settling down—it's all to ensure they never have to lay eyes on me again. If the marines had let me…" he drew a jagged breath

"...I would've stayed in Afghanistan until the job was done."

Unable to bear the pain he was enduring on his own, Tara tentatively put a hand out on the table. Waiting. It was there if he needed it.

"You do know none of this was your fault, don't you?"

Collapsing his head into his hands again, she could just make out his voice. "I know. I know. I've been over it countless times. There was nothing else I could do. It was protocol."

"So why do you hold yourself accountable?" She asked the question, knowing the answer. Knowing she would've felt the same way had she been in his shoes.

Still speaking through his hands, he replied, "He was my brother. He was my brother and saving him should have been the priority." He looked up, blue eyes darkening with emotion. "Now I just need to find a way to live with myself. Staying out of what's left of my family's way and living on the move has worked pretty well so far."

"So far?" Tara couldn't keep the curiosity out of her voice.

"Can't you see? Everything's changed now."

Fraser dropped his hands away from his face. How the man could still look this ruggedly handsome in the midst of his grief was beyond her, and it took everything in Tara's power not to leap across the table and hold him, kiss him—to just let him know he wasn't alone.

Just friends, remember.

"Changed how?"

He met her gaze with a look of pure and open honesty. "Tara...I've met you."

Tears sprang to Tara's eyes. Could her whole world have truly changed in an instant? What exactly was it that Fraser was trying to say? One thing was for sure, she didn't know if she was ready for the powerful waves of emotion he unleashed in her. The past year or so had been an oasis of calm. A much-needed recovery after her ex had ripped everything out from under her feet. Now here was a man, an incredibly gorgeous man no less, who made her feel about as feminine and sexy as a woman could. Not to mention a man who selflessly championed her work when he had nothing to gain. And he was promising... what, exactly?

Not a thing. And she needed to remember that.

Even though it hurt so much to know she could never tell him how much she loved him. For, despite her best efforts, she was head over heels in love with Fraser MacKenzie and it was going to take every ounce of energy she possessed to keep it in check.

Fraser waved a hand over the elaborate meals left untouched on their plates. Forcing out a half-hearted laugh, he said, "I'm doing a pretty good job of ensuring we don't get a bite to eat, aren't I?"

Tara offered him a soft smile and waved dismissively. "Not to worry. I wasn't that hungry."

"What?" He put on an expression of mock fury. "After I've gone to all this effort? I've spent the entire day slaving away over a hot stove to create this incredible meal for you!"

Tara couldn't help but laugh along with him. She knew as well as he did that the lodge chefs were the only ones who could take credit for their rapidly cooling dinners. She might not know a lot, but she did know that she'd underestimated Fraser. There was so much more to him than a slick set of one-liners and an insanely handsome exterior. The fact that he'd been through such a life-changing trauma in Afghanistan and still put himself second in everything—during the avalanche, the rescue, in coping with losing Eric.

He amazed her. After yesterday's ordeal he'd still come back up fighting and now here he was telling her—what exactly? *That she could trust him?* Her mind careened from point to point, trying to find a way to believe him. Her heart wanted so very much to take the risk—to have a shot at loving him. Even the idea of loving Fraser thrilled and terrified her at the same time. It was an emotional step she hadn't planned on taking again.

Suddenly feeling the need to relieve the tension thick in the air, Tara jumped up from her chair, making comedy tiptoe steps in the direction of the pies on the nearby table. "Do you think anyone would mind if we popped these in a box, went next door, put on an old film and ate a pie each?"

Fraser looked at her, his heart flooding with relief. How could this woman know him so well when just a few weeks ago they'd been complete strangers? Confessing his history to her had been exhausting. He'd never shared so much with anyone before and it had taken a physical toll. There was no energy left in him to hash out the ramifications of what he had done. Or to take on board the fact that Tara might not want him now she knew the real reason behind his seemingly cavalier attitude to settling down. Yet there she was, his perfect woman, beckoning him to join her.

Wild horses couldn't keep him away. Just being with her gave him a sense of calm. The sense of peace he had been searching the globe for these last few years. Who'd have known he'd find it here in little old Deer Creek?

Fraser pushed himself up from the table, accepting Tara's invitation to join her in her apartment with a grin.

So much had been said tonight. So much to absorb. For both of them. A quiet night next to the woman he was falling madly in love with was exactly what the doctor ordered. Correction. He'd *fallen* in love—taking the tumble was hardly an order, it was a miracle.

"What do you fancy? A comedy or a thriller?" Tara grinned up at Fraser as she waggled a couple of DVD boxes in front of him as options.

"How about a romance?" He closed the small space between them with a single stride, suddenly quite certain that watching a movie was the last thing on his mind.

"What?" She looked up at him incredulously. "I didn't think you menfolk went for that sort of thing."

"Depends upon what form the romance takes," Fraser plucked the DVDs out of her hands and put them on a side table then put out a hand for her to join him on the sofa.

Tara's expression shifted, a flash of understanding turning swiftly to her head shaking in an agitated no-way-buster move. "No. I can't. No... I mean yes... I want to, I can't tell you how much I want to...but, Fraser—"

Fraser pulled her into his arms, holding her gently, his voice barely audible in the quiet winter's night. The backs of his fingers stroked her cheek as he confessed, "Tara, I'm in love with you. I'm so very much in love with you."

For an instant the whole world froze in place. Tara held her breath, her eyes flashing up to his to see how much truth was behind them. She'd wanted to hear those words so very badly and could hardly believe she was hearing them now. "But you'll be going—"

"Maybe, maybe not. As I said, in meeting you, everything has changed."

Tara felt Fraser's finger draw her chin up towards him, his lips an excruciatingly close distance from her own. Her body was alight with desire. She lowered her gaze, dropping her eyes to rest on his lips. She caught her breath as he wove a hand through her hair and gently pulled her head back, exposing her throat.

Tara could hardly bear how unbelievably feminine she felt as he held her close, a long forefinger beginning to trace a path along her lower lip. She felt her lips respond to his touch, a tremble of longing flooding down her spine—a longing so deep-seeded she could scarcely breathe. In an instant she was accepting and responding to the deep kisses Fraser began giving her. She felt her entire body relieve itself of any vow of chastity she had made in the past. She wanted him, had wanted him from the instant she'd seen him, and now he loved her. *He loved her!*

As kisses rained down on her mouth, her throat, she felt her own hands and mouth begin to make tentative explorations. Her fingers slipped up his chest and pulled his shoulders towards her with a newfound confidence. *Fraser MacKenzie loved her.* Fire surged through her as she allowed herself to enjoy caressing his neck, the well-defined strength of his back. Her fingers felt as though they were finally allowed to explore and enjoy a long-forbidden temptation.

She felt Fraser's hands slip towards her waist, thumbs grazing her breasts as he made his physical claim on her. Each of his touches pushed her further into the realms of a heightened awareness she hadn't imagined possible. Her legs lost all strength as her lips moved in passionate harmony with his. She could barely think. Didn't want to think.

Her breasts pressed into him as if she weren't able to get close enough. A low groan escaped her throat as she felt her nipples responding to the well-muscled proportions of his chest. A taut internal ache teased her nipples to form into tight buds against the lace of her bra. It wasn't just her breasts that were responding to him, that desired him. Every pore in her body craved more. It was as if she was feeling her body anew. Thoughts fluttered in and out of her mind but nothing stuck. With each of Fraser's caresses heat flooded throughout her—electric, jolting, volcanic heat.

His lips took hold of hers, one by one. Giving each a gentle nibble, a light flick of the tongue, he teased her until she had to restrain a whimper from forming, when suddenly he dove back into her mouth and with a swift move lifted her off the floor, wrapped her legs around his hips and kissed her with a level of sensual pleasure she had never imagined possible. She was barely aware they'd crossed from the living room into the bedroom until he laid her down upon her bed, lowering himself beside her.

"Fraser, are we—?"

She felt his finger drag across her swollen lips to silence her.

"Tonight. I don't want you to think about anything but tonight."

Tara nestled comfortably into the warm folds of her duvet, letting out a little sigh of contentment. Something felt different. Something—no, someone—was missing from her bed. She cracked open one eye, then the other, realizing pretty quickly she was alone.

Pressing herself up into a seated position, she scanned the room. What was going on?

A flurry of memories snapped her wide awake. The last thing she remembered was being held in Fraser's arms after a ridiculously perfect night of lovemaking. It was as if he'd unleashed a side of her she'd never known existed before now. The night had been unbelievably magical. Better than she'd ever let herself imagine in the handful of moments she'd allowed herself to daydream.

Cocking her head to the side, she listened carefully. No creaking floorboards, no sounds other than the odd hoot of an owl. It was still dark out. A quick glance at her clock and she saw that it was only just past five in the morning. Fraser was an early bird but she hadn't thought he liked to be up this early.

Tara heard a sound coming from the kitchen. What was it? A second, louder, gurgly noise spluttered forth from the kitchen.

Pulling the duvet away from her legs, Tara slipped her feet to the cold floor. Coffee too? *He's good!*

Quickly padding across the living room, she entered the kitchen. Empty.

Propped against the percolating coffee pot was a turkey-shaped gingerbread cookie and a handwritten note. A smile flew to her lips as she noted Fraser would definitely fall into the category of doctors whose penmanship nurses despaired over. At least it made him a bit more human. Her eyes ran over the scrawled script in a flash.

Morning, Dorothy—had to leave. The Tin Man

Tara's heart lurched into her throat, her fingers flying to her neck as if to stop the constriction of breath.

Go where and for how long? And *the Tin Man*? The Tin Man didn't have a heart! What on earth was Fraser trying to say?

Heartless was the polar opposite of how Tara would have described Fraser, a man who'd whirled into her life like a tornado. A mind-blowingly gorgeous, not to mention medically impressive, tornado. Was he leaving Deer Creek? Leaving her? Or did he just have to leave to get milk or something? *What sort of message was this?*

Lowering herself into the breakfast nook, Tara felt her mouth go dry with panic. She forced herself to take even breaths. She been such an idiot to believe for a second she could trust Fraser.

Something told her this wasn't Fraser just whizzing out to run an errand. He was leaving for good.

She wasn't anywhere near Kansas and Deer Creek was no Oz, but Tara knew in her sinking heart that Deer Creek would never be the same without Fraser MacKenzie in it. She didn't know why, but an ever-increasing ache in her gut was telling her she'd seen the last of him.

Strictly speaking, it wasn't a farewell note, but last night's confession over dinner should have served as fair warning. Fraser didn't like to stick around, particularly when emotions were involved. He saw himself as the man responsible for the death of his brother and for orphaning his niece and nephew. It was a heavy load to handle and perhaps running away from commitment was the only way he would ever be able to deal with his grief, the only way to avoid losing someone else he cared about. *He'd told her he loved her!*

She abruptly crumpled up his note and stuffed it in the trash. Tears stung at her eyes as she felt fury well up within her. Fury that she had let herself back into the emotional no-go zone. A zone she'd created for exactly this sort of scenario. Rejection.

"At least he made coffee," she muttered to the empty room.

Wait a minute! Her heart lurched again.

Did the percolating coffee-maker mean he'd just been here? Did she still have a chance to catch him and demand an explanation? He owed her that at the very least. How dare he just whirl into her life, make mincemeat of her heart then leave town as though she had meant absolutely nothing to him? Not to mention all the patients he would be abandoning.

Now she was properly fuming. *How dare he?* How dare he leave her in a professional lurch like this?

She exhaled a bitter laugh.

What had she expected? She'd been a fool to succumb to his well-practiced charms. It was back to being the lone wolf. Just the way she liked it.

* * *

Fraser glanced at his watch. Anxiety actively gnawed at his nerves as each box was filled, taped and labeled. He'd hardly let himself move in, so moving on was relatively easy. Well, physically. Emotionally? That was a whole different ballgame.

He sat back on his heels and scanned the room. Not much left. The condo already had the same empty feel it had the day he'd moved in. Leaving like this, leaving Tara like this, was the last thing he wanted to do, but he was sure he was doing the best thing. For both of them.

He stepped up to the picture windows facing the resort. Christmas trees twinkled away in the lodge. The lights and seasonal decorations wound their way along the main street up into the hillside, where a handful of houses etched another line of Christmas cheer along the edges of Deer Creek. Houses full of families anticipating the big day.

He took a step back and continued with his packing. He couldn't remember the last Christmas he'd spent as part of a family. His niece and nephew had hardly been old enough to spell when he'd seen them last.

He shook away the memory of his brother's family gathered around their Christmas tree the final time they'd been home on leave together.

Avoiding the holiday entirely had proved a fairly effective technique until now. All of the other resorts had been more than happy to accommodate his request that he be scheduled to work Christmas. And now?

He took a cursory glance around the increasingly bare living room. Christmas Eve was around the corner and it was time to move on.

CHAPTER TEN

"LIESEL, COULD YOU send in the next patient, please?"

Tara hung up the intercom phone, irritated with herself for not wanting to go out into the waiting room like she normally did.

She just didn't have the strength. Not today. Given that Liesel had just lost the love of her life and was out there facing the general public made her feel pretty pathetic. Hearing the doorknob turn, she pushed herself round in her chair to face her next patient.

The hint of a smile she had forced onto her lips disappeared in an instant. Fraser MacKenzie and his six-foot-something perfect self filled her doorway.

"I'm sorry, we only deal with emergencies here."

"Tara, I know what you must be thinking—"

"No. You don't have the slightest idea what I'm

thinking and that's exactly how I'd like to keep it. If you'll excuse me, I've got real patients to attend to." Tara gestured for him to leave. The door was still standing ajar. As she willed him to turn round and go, her heart burned for him to stay, to declare his love for her again. But that bridge had been burnt and would never be crossed again.

"Tara, just give me two minutes. I know I don't deserve it, but I can't go without making sure you understand I never lied to you."

"What about?" Her eyes blazed with fury as she pushed herself up from her chair. "The fact that, no matter what, you'll never settle down? The fact you prefer a one-off with a snow bunny to a genuine relationship? Or the fact that you loved me for one night only?"

Pain darkened Fraser's eyes to a dark, churning blue. "Tara, I never, ever meant to disrespect you. Never."

"Then why did you lie?" She shot back. "Why mention the one thing you knew I was terrified to hear?"

"It's not as if you returned the sentiment." His words sounded hollow, empty—as if he had already left and it was a hologram standing there in her office, making a mockery of her.

Tara's mind raced back to the previous night. *Had she told him she loved him?* She knew she felt it. Despite her every vow not to, she loved Fraser more than she had imagined possible, but had she said it out loud? She couldn't remember. "So wait a minute. You're leaving Deer Creek because I didn't say I loved you? How could you not know it was true? Not know I wouldn't have let things progress so...so intimately if I didn't love you."

"It doesn't matter now." Fraser dropped his eyes from hers, the tone of his voice becoming more distant than she could have imagined possible. "It's too soon. For both of us."

Hot spikes of anger shot through her. "How dare you decide what is too soon for me? I make the decisions about my life and who I love. Not you!"

"The same holds true for me, Tara. And this isn't right for me. Not right now." Fraser shook his head slowly, as if trying to convince himself the words he was saying were true. "Look, I've organized cover for a few days. I need time to sort myself out—figure out what my options are. A couple of guys from the Valley ER said they'd stand in for me. I'll be in touch. You've got a good group of people around you, Tara. They're all looking out for you."

Before she could get a word in edgeways, he was gone. Just as quickly as he'd arrived in her life, Fraser MacKenzie left, having taken the one thing she'd thought she'd never give away again. Her *heart*.

Tara raised a mittened hand, mixed emotions coursing through her. She waved a reluctant fare-well until the blue four-by-four carrying Liesel and all her luggage down to the Valley disappeared from sight.

"They'll look after her."

Tara gave a start. She'd been so engrossed in Liesel's departure she hadn't heard Marian approach. Tara offered her a weak smile.

"I know. Eric's family are good people." She felt herself choking back a few tears. "It still doesn't seem real, does it?"

"Seven months is a long time to sort out a plan, honey."

Just the thought of Liesel's pregnancy painfully compressed Tara's heart. "I suppose. Still, if she goes back to Australia, it'll be hard for Eric's parents."

Marian put a reassuring arm around Tara's shoulder. "Don't you worry, Tara. Deer Creek takes care of its own. You and all other members of our extended family will be looked after. We'll see to that."

Tara avoided the kindly baker's gaze after the barely veiled reference to Fraser. Or was it? It was hard to tell. Despite herself, every single thought she had led straight back to Fraser. After their Thanksgiving meal she had thought—no, she had hoped—he'd really meant those cherished words. *I love you.* She'd been so very naïve to believe him.

Her eyes stung with the injustice of it all. In just a few short weeks he had become the person who was always there for her. The person she knew she could share a laugh with or consult with on a professional matter. Now, in one heartbreaking swoop, she had lost him and now Liesel. Not that she resented Liesel's decision to go.

Eric's family had offered to take her in to stay

with them in the Valley even before they had heard about her unexpected pregnancy. It would be easy enough to find a replacement nurse and being up on the mountain right now was too hard for her.

Since the news that Liesel was carrying Eric Hunter's baby had become common knowledge, Tara had watched with admiration as the whole of Deer Creek, and many families from the Valley, had united in offering the Hunter family and Liesel countless pies, casseroles, firewood—anything that would help ease the pain. The funeral had been held straight away and the rich outpouring of love and support that had followed had been truly moving to witness.

Tara had always felt welcomed and happy over the past year at Deer Creek, but now she genuinely felt as though she was part of a community. A community that supported people individually and came together as an unbeatable unit in times of crisis and joy. It seemed clear that, despite his best efforts, Fraser could not see himself as a part of the community here. Or, perhaps, he *would* not. It had already been forty-seven hours since she had last seen him and still no word.

She linked arms with Marian, giving the older woman's arm a squeeze. She needed a distraction from her thoughts about Fraser. "I don't suppose you have any of your holiday pecan rolls left, do you?"

A broad smile was all the answer she needed.

"And where are you transiting to today, sir?" The British passport control officer smiled at him as if taking yet another long-haul flight even further away from Tara was a good thing.

"Kenya...Nairobi." Flying back to England to get a transit flight to Kenya was the plan. A trial run with Médecins Sans Frontières was the perfect anecdote to the six-month contract usually required for a ski season. Finishing the four months he had left at Deer Creek was out of the question.

He couldn't have messed that up more if he'd planned it. It'd be tricky finding a replacement at this point in the season, but he had enough phone numbers to call, enough favors owed. And whatever he'd inflicted upon Tara emotionally, he certainly wasn't going to leave her in the lurch professionally. He owed her that at the very least.

He scanned the departures lounge filled with people heading for sun-soaked vacations and business meetings. He was eager to join the focused flow of travelers. Crisis management for refugees. Always on the move. *Perfect.*

His eyes flicked to the departures board. Nairobi…Nairobi… There it was: delayed—for five hours.

No. He needed to keep moving. Sitting still for the nine-hour flight across the Atlantic had been hard enough. Quashing thoughts of Tara's face when she'd realised he was going had been torture. If he wanted to know what hate looked like, he was pretty sure he'd had a good sneak preview.

So sitting around at the airport for a few more hours before another long plane journey that played a non-stop run of romantic comedies? Out of the question. He couldn't just sit there and wait. He needed to do something. His eyes tracked across the activity of the departures lounge again. In just a matter of moments it seemed to have taken on an entirely different atmosphere.

Suddenly everyone just seemed part of a huge disconnection. Hundreds of people scurrying here and there, looking up at the flight times, speeding to gates, racing for…what? New beginnings? Escape from the past? How many flights had he boarded over the years? How many continents had he traveled to, hoping to leave the past behind him? The scene sprawled before him suddenly turned his stomach with disgust. No matter how you painted it, he was running away. Again.

Fraser picked up his small overnight bag and headed towards passport control. He knew what he had to do. It had been long enough. *You call yourself a man, Fraser MacKenzie? Well, prove it.*

Tara picked each of the blueberries out of her pancakes and started to form them into a happy face on the vandalized pancake. Reconsidering, she abruptly turned the smile into a frown. She took a swig of her cinnamon latte. Nope. That wasn't very nice this morning either. This was the worst beginning to Christmas Eve ever.

Fraser's absence had now stretched beyond the "few days" prediction. Why hadn't he just been upfront with her and simply said he wasn't returning? That she meant nothing to him. This waiting game was beginning to verge on cruel.

The days were hard enough to get through and surviving her sleepless nights had long since taken its toll. She'd been through her old movie collection and finally put a halt to it when she'd realized she was watching the credits roll for *Pride and Prejudice* for the third time. There was only so much Mr. Darcy a girl could take.

Her apartment had been thoroughly cleaned. Twice. All her Christmas presents had been purchased, wrapped and labeled. She'd even laid them out below the small tree her apartment could only just contain. Then rearranged them. More than once.

Anger had turned into worry as Fraser's absence from the clinic morphed from a few days to ten. Two hundred and forty incredibly long hours. *Not that she was counting.*

"I don't think I've ever seen someone look so miserable over a plate of pancakes before." Marian plonked herself down in the worn leather chair across from Tara without an invitation.

It was all Tara could do not to scowl at her friend, but now wasn't the time for chitchat. If she started to explain why she had a face like thunder it would probably turn into a rainstorm. Crying in the middle of Marian's bakery was hardly the behavior of the resort doctor.

"Oh, it's nothing really. I just haven't been sleeping much. And the clinic's been really busy."

"C'mon, honey." Marian gave her shoulder a reassuring pat. "It's only me. It's your Doc Mackenzie, isn't it?"

Tara felt her face drain of color. Was she wearing a sign that made it that obvious? "How'd you know?"

"Honey, everybody knows."

Tara dropped her fork as if it were a hot poker. If she hadn't felt like eating her maple-syrup-drowned pancakes before, she really didn't feel like eating them now. *How humiliating.* The whole of Deer Creek knew she'd been mooning over the unattainable and runaway doctor who'd made it clear from the beginning he wasn't the type to stick around?

Marian lowered her voice but continued in the same comforting tone, "My dear, from the moment that man walked into the bakery I knew you two were a match. Don't ask me how I knew, but having seen the pair of you over the past few weeks it hasn't taken too many investigative skills to see you're both lovesick."

Tara lowered her head into her hands, hoping to hide some of the color rushing to her cheeks. This was absolutely mortifying. Through the muffling of her fingers she allowed the words to be said out loud, "But he's gone. And it's Christmas Eve!" It was all Tara could do to not let her admission form into a wail. She knew she'd fallen for Fraser. Head over heels, like a bewitched teenager. Her ears were ringing with the cacophony of thoughts battling for attention in her head.

Where had he gone?

Why had he gone?

Was it because of what had happened at the hospital with Eric?

Or was it because he had finally given himself a glimpse of happiness, security, by admitting that he loved her and felt she didn't feel the same way? She could've kicked herself again and again for not shouting out to the hills at that very moment that she loved him too. Of course she loved him.

And, more importantly, why, why, why had he

done this at Christmas? She adored Christmas. Everyone knew that. Even though Fraser had obviously realized he didn't love her enough, surely he respected her enough to wait until after the holiday to ruin her life.

"Uh-oh, honey, you'd better come with me to the back."

"Why?" Tara pulled her tear-stained face from out of her hands and followed Marian's startled glance out at the main street.

A combination of rage and despair churned round her stomach. There was Fraser, looking happy as a clam, walking down Main Street with a beautiful blonde woman on his arm. They were laughing, heads bent close together as if sharing a private joke. It was all Tara could do to remember to breathe.

Instead of responding to Marian's insistent tugging on her arm, Tara remained cemented to the spot. *Seriously?* He had someone new? Not that she'd been his "someone old". Or perhaps, like with her ex, Fraser had been playing her all along. Fraser was the one who told her quite openly about his reputation as the Smooth Operator. She had known he had no credentials of longevity, of commitment. She must've been crazy to think he'd want to stay here in Deer Creek. With her. Forever.

"I think you've seen enough, honey. Let's get you to the clinic out the back."

"Absolutely," Tara shot back defiantly. "If I never see Fraser MacKenzie again, it will be too soon."

"So you really think you'll be happy here?"

Fraser nodded enthusiastically, almost surprised at his own response to his sister-in-law's question. He felt happy. Genuinely happy. He'd done a "typical Fraser" and fled the scene as soon as possible after his incredible evening with Tara. When she'd fallen asleep in his arms that night, he had felt so responsible for her. It had been too much. Too much to take in in the wake of everything he'd lost. He did not deserve the level of compassion and care she had shown him—the trust. And then he'd gone and made her feel like it had been her fault he'd left. Thank heavens Julie had knocked some sense into him.

"Here, I want to show you the house. I need a woman's opinion on what I've done with it. Then we'll go and get the kids from their ski lesson and maybe rearrange the furniture if you think it could be better." He couldn't believe he was fretting this much. It was just a house.

No. That wasn't right. This was his home. The home he hoped he would share with Tara if… It was a pretty big *if.* He hadn't exactly been the most consistent of suitors.

"So, let me get this straight." Julie turned from the house to catch him in the beams of an approving smile. "You abandoned Tara with pretty much no explanation at all. Now, courtesy of the internet and an obliging real estate agent, you've bought this incredibly beautiful Craftsman House in the hope you can prove you're in this for the real deal?"

"Right."

"Got it." She cocked a dubious eyebrow at him.

"What? I'm a romantic!" He protested. Julie's doubtful expression remained unchanged. "I've been spontaneous before."

Julie howled with laughter, giving Fraser a yeah-sure-buddy pat on the shoulder. "Fraser MacKenzie, the most romantic thing I've ever seen you do is, uhhhmmmm…" Julie paused theatrically to try and come up with an answer. Fraser batted away her teasing barbs, suddenly feeling the need to prove to his sister-in-law that he was good for this. He was in it for the long haul.

Reaching into his pocket, he pulled out the little black box he'd picked up before collecting Julie and the kids at the airport. He opened the lid and was gratified with the gasp of admiration Julie gave. "How does this grab you for a "real deal" proposal?"

"It's absolutely beautiful, Fraser." She looked up at him with tears in her eyes. "I know I haven't met her yet, but she'd be a fool to say no. Your brother would be over the moon to know you'd found such happiness."

"Julie, I…" Fraser was at a loss. Again. This was precisely why he'd been running around the globe like a lost wanderer for the past few years. Julie and Matt had been his pinup couple for a perfect marriage. His parents had had a great marriage, but Julie and Matt had genuinely been best friends as well. It was the type of relationship Fraser had thought he would never deserve. Until now. He wanted to spend the rest of his days earning his place by Tara's side. If she could forgive him.

"Look, big brother-in-law. It's like I told you back in the UK, I knew when I married a military man what risks Matt would be taking and what that meant for me and our family. Matt will forever be my hero. He died doing what he believed was good and true and I can never..." She paused to lock eyes with Fraser to emphasize her point. "I can never begrudge losing him for doing what he thought was right. And I have never, not once, held you responsible. Now, stop wandering around town with me and go and get your girl."

Fraser pulled Julie into a deep bear hug. She was an amazing woman. Resting his head on top of Julie's as their tight hug relaxed, he welcomed the wash of peace that came over him as he gazed at the newly furnished living room.

He felt a smile tug at his lips as he and Julie drew apart and smiled at the room together. The furniture was almost incidental. At the center of the golden hardwood floor of the living room was the most perfect Christmas tree he'd been able to find. There were now just a handful of hours before he found out if Tara would accept his proposal.

* * *

Tara looked at the pieces of the stale gingerbread house she'd broken to bits on her examination table. Crabbily she picked one up, discarded it and selected another for inspection. Begrudgingly, she had to admit the chocolate discs were delicious. Dark chocolate was surely every girl's cure-all.

Sighing, she sank back into her chair, feeling utterly deflated. It was the end of a long day—Christmas Eve was always a bit wild on the slopes. Everyone was in high gear for the holidays and adrenaline rushes on the mountainside equaled injuries. Fortunately, there hadn't been anything too severe and she'd been working with one of the temporary nurses from Valley Hospital who had easily helped her wade through the morning and afternoon flurries of patients.

The nurse had gone now and the clinic was technically closed for the day, but Tara was feeling listless and the last thing she wanted to do was go up into her apartment. It would remind her of everything she didn't have to celebrate. She had half-heartedly decked her very small hall and made a stab at embellishing the decorations Fraser had left at her house after Thanksgiving.

Thanksgiving. The night with Fraser played through her mind again and again. So many unanswered questions. She squished her eyes shut as tightly as she could then opened them wide— neither was a particularly successful method of ridding her head of images of the Scottish Don Juan who had crushed her heart.

Going to her apartment was definitely an option. Then again, leaving the clinic would mean the possibility of running into Fraser and the Other Woman. Deer Creek was a small place and Tara wasn't going to risk another sighting of he-who-shall-not-be-named.

She was unable to resist a sardonic laugh. *Absolutely perfect.* Just when she'd thought her life had really started to take shape here—her research back in her hands, the full support of the hospital behind her, her heart bursting with love— Fraser, the man of her dreams, had morphed into the Grinch who'd stolen her beloved Christmas. Absolutely rich as fruit cake.

There was no doubt about it. The impact his absence was going to have on her life seemed a pretty surefire route to spinsterhood. No. Lone wolf. Far more attractive. Spinsters wept and wolves howled. Right now she felt like howling.

Finding the remains of the gingerbread house lacking, Tara decided to head for the staff refrigerator. Maybe there was some eggnog in there she'd missed. Eggnog always made things a little bit nicer. *Even if you were busy hating the man who had taken your heart and pulverized it into a thousand tiny pieces.*

"Medic One, this is Ski Patrol Three. Do you read me, over?"

Tara lurched across the counter to grab the radio. Good. *Something to preoccupy me.* "This is Medic One, I read you. Over."

"We're coming by in about two minutes to take you to a code red over on Deer Creek Lane. Just bring your standard kit. Over."

"That's fine. See you in two. Over."

Tara scrunched up her face in confusion. She wasn't normally called out to the residential sites and the ski patroller had sounded strangely relaxed for a code red. She was, of course, more than happy to help. Perhaps, owing to the fact it was Christmas Eve, she was the only option. A twist of pain captured her breath for a moment. *Well.* The only doctor who had any staying power, anyway.

As if by rote, she pulled on her all-weather coat, hat and gloves, and shouldered the backpack that held a self-contained medical kit. Instinct told her she shouldn't call an ambulance as backup. Not yet. As soon as the medic arrived and she got a full report, she'd make the call.

Pulling the clinic door shut behind her, Tara turned at the sound of the snowmobile.

Shivers of emotion sent goose-bumps racing up her arms.

The figure riding the snowmobile looked all too familiar. Her heart leapt and just as quickly began to pump so rapidly her ears filled with a painful roar. It was all Tara could do not to turn around and walk straight back into the clinic. She forced herself to hold her ground as he pulled to a smooth halt beside her.

There he was. Fraser MacKenzie. Sitting on his snowmobile, looking at her as if he hadn't been away for more than five minutes.

"Jump on, m'lady."

"Helmet." Tara put out a gloved hand, fastidiously avoiding looking into those deep blue eyes that never failed to turn her into a weak-kneed mess. If there hadn't been a patient waiting, she'd be gone.

"Oh, dear. Someone's not in a very Christmassy mood."

"I wonder why."

Fraser handed her a helmet, eyes briefly squinting as if to divine an answer. "I wasn't scheduled today, was I? I thought I'd organized cover for the past few—"

"No," Tara bit out, cutting him off. "Today's shift was my distinct pleasure, as it has been for the past ten days, thank you very much."

"Well, we'd best get going."

Tara climbed onto the back of the snowmobile, ruing the seating arrangement. She tried sitting upright on the seat, avoiding putting her arms around Fraser, but judging by the speedy departure he was clearly in no mood to hang around. Gritting her teeth she moved her arms forward, forced to hold onto him to keep her grip on the seat.

Unbelievable. First he tears my heart in two and now he's trying to kill me. Merry Christmas, everyone!

* * *

"You all right back there?" Fraser called back over his shoulder, aware he might've been a bit quick on the accelerator. He was running on adrenaline.

"Fine."

Tara's reply was terse. He didn't blame her. This whole exercise was well and truly testing fate. Their fate.

"Good, good. We should be there in a few minutes."

"What's the code red?"

"Oh. I think it might be a yellow," Fraser fudged. He'd already forgotten the back story he'd had the ski patroller at the Blue Lantern make up to get her out of the clinic. He'd been lucky the patroller had been willing to break protocol and play along with the ruse at all. Revving the snowmobile up a notch, Fraser focused on getting past Main Street and making the snowy hill climb ahead of them. He just had to hold out for a few more blocks.

Tara glowered as they swept along Main Street, where the shop windows were twinkling away merrily. All the lights, decorations and holiday preparations she had always seen as a beautiful communal expression of the Christmas spirit passed in a blur. Pressed against Fraser as she was, it was impossible not to allow herself a surreptitious inhalation of his scent. A personal aroma her body was organically drawn to. She felt a physical ache, a need to lay her head against his back, feel the warmth spread from his body to hers as he manipulated the snowmobile through the snowy trenches. Not now. *Not any more.*

Steeling herself, Tara kept herself as separate from Fraser's body as she could. He was the last person she wanted to desire and the sooner this callout was over, the better.

She watched silently as they passed the resort and climbed the hill to a small residential area. A smattering of houses facing out towards the valley that Tara had daydreamed about living in one day. There was one in particular...

"I thought no one lived here."

Tara jumped off of the back of the snowmobile in front of the deep green Craftsman. The "For Sale" sign she'd been eagle-eyeing over the past few months was noticeably absent. Warm light glowed from large wooden-framed windows nestled snugly along one of the most inviting porches Deer Creek had on offer.

"No one does."

"I don't have time for riddles, Fraser. Where's the patient?"

"You're looking at him."

Tara took a step back, trying to control the swell of ire she felt growing within her. What was he talking about?

"Look, Fraser. I'm not in the mood to be messed around. Not tonight. Just go find your little blonde snow bunny and she can give you all the TLC you need."

Fraser looked as if she had slapped him.

"Tara, I don't know what you think you saw…"

It was too late to change her mind now. Christmas or no Christmas, she might as well have it out with him and then say goodbye. "You know exactly what I saw. You must think I'm an idiot. An empty chalet, you looking as happy as can be, with a blonde woman dangling off your arm. You warned me you were a bit of a Lothario, but I hadn't realized that abandoning the clinic in order to charm your way through the residents of

Deer Creek was your style." Tara had more but stopped in mid-rant as a broad smile began to unfurl on Fraser's lips and he began to chuckle.

"Why are you laughing at me?" She was about as close to stamping her feet as she had ever come.

"Why, Dr. Braxton," he drawled, his brogue lazily working its way across the "r" in her name, "I think you just might be jealous."

Tara bridled. Fraser may have just called a spade a spade but he was certainly the last person on earth who was going to know the truth. "Don't be ridiculous. I need someone I can rely on and you are certainly not *it*. Consider yourself freed from any contract we have. Professional or otherwise."

Fraser took a step towards her, his six-foot-plus frame making its usual impressive presence. Tara felt her body shift into its intuitive pulse-quickening state of sensual response to the sheer masculinity of him. *Does he really have to put me through this?*

"Actually, I brought you here tonight to discuss an entirely different type of contract."

Tara's head felt as if it was spinning. What was

he trying to say? Was he going to stay here in her dream house with the woman she'd seen him with? The thought was unbearable.

"Spit it out, Fraser. I'd like to get back to my real patients."

Extending a hand towards her, Fraser maintained his broad smile. Tara firmly stuffed her gloved hands into her pockets, fighting the primal urge to put her hand in his.

"All right, then, if you want to play it that way…"

Before she could protest, Fraser had closed the space between them in a split second, scooped her up into his arms and carried her up the steps of the porch. "I had hoped this wouldn't happen under duress," he murmured into her ear, as her arms sought purchase round his neck.

Words escaped Tara as the intimacy of his touch soaked into her like a soothing tonic. *Putty.* Despite her best efforts she was actually like putty in his hands. He slipped her to the wooden planked floor of the porch as if she weighed no more than a feather.

Tara watched incredulously as Fraser lowered himself to one knee to the porch, taking both of her hands in his. Heat shot up her arms, coiling in a fluid rush of sensation charging her entire body.

"Tara Braxton, meeting you has changed my world. Being with you has taught me the most important thing is to live life as richly as I can." Tara caught her breath, barely able to acknowledge this wasn't a dream.

"I believe," Fraser continued, as he pulled out a small black box, "life partners should bring out the very best in the other and you, Tara Braxton, bring out the very best in me. Will you do me the honor of becoming my wife?"

Tara drew in a sharp breath as Fraser opened the lid to the box to reveal a beautiful solitaire ring.

"But…" Tara faltered. "You moved out. I saw you with another woman."

"I moved out so I—we—could move here! It didn't take much of a genius to figure out the real estate agent's details on the staff refrigerator were there for a reason. A bit more digging and I heard you had been asking about this property. When you told me you could buy the practice or the house, I thought that after all you'd been through with your ex, you more than deserved your own practice. A place that would serve as the nerve center for all your innovations. I bought this to prove to you I can stay somewhere. That I *want* to stay somewhere. Here. With you." Fraser continued at high speed, afraid he couldn't get it all out if he let Tara speak.

"The woman you saw is my sister-in-law. Julie. She and the kids can't wait to meet you." He was serious now, holding her gaze steadily. "There were some old ghosts I needed to lay to rest. Having her here to meet you—the woman I love— was one of the steps I needed to take. Besides, she helped me pick out a few bits of furniture to make moving in with me a bit more of a desirable option..." Fraser threw back his head and laughed as Tara stared at him wordlessly. He pressed her hands together in his. "How about an answer?"

"Do you mean it? All of it?"

"Of course I do, Tara. I love you. And I plan on loving you a very, very long time."

"Well, then—" Tara eyed him mischievously, certain in her heart he was speaking the truth

"—as long as it is a very, very long time then, yes! Of course, yes! I love you, too."

In an instant Fraser was on his feet, his parted lips capturing Tara's mouth with his own. She hungrily returned his kisses, her senses on overdrive. She felt his fingers slide through her hair, his thumbs tracing their way along her jaw. Simultaneously tender and possessive, she felt her body finally give in to the full tumultuous swing of sensations Fraser brought out in her. All of them better than she could have imagined. Her hands wove together behind his neck as she felt herself being lifted off the porch and swung around, Fraser still claiming the countless kisses she willingly gave.

Tara threw back her head and laughed with pure unadulterated joy as he opened the door with his spare hand and carried her into the house.

"Next time I do this, you'll be in a wedding dress."

"Next time you do this, you'll have enjoyed much more than a thank-you kiss," Tara whispered into his ear as she slid her legs down those well-muscled thighs to the parquet floor.

"Promise?" Fraser husked.

"Oh, you can count on it." Her eyes twinkled back at him with a look that vowed to come good on her promise many times over before their wedding day.

Turning Tara to face the living room, Fraser wrapped his arms around her from behind. She gasped at the sight of the most beautifully decorated Christmas tree she'd ever laid eyes on. Entwining her fingers with his, she could hardly breathe as she took in the elegant décor, the ornaments reflecting the gentle glow of hundreds of delicate lights laced through the branches. If she had done it herself, she couldn't have done it better. It was perfect. Just the idea that she would get to spend Christmas after Christmas here with Fraser brought tears to her eyes.

She felt him lean down to kiss away her tears. "I don't know what to say, Fraser."

"Merry Christmas, Mrs. Almost-MacKenzie."

"Well, my love, a very merry Christmas to you."

* * * * *

MILLS & BOON®
Large Print Medical

May

PLAYING THE PLAYBOY'S SWEETHEART	Carol Marinelli
UNWRAPPING HER ITALIAN DOC	Carol Marinelli
A DOCTOR BY DAY...	Emily Forbes
TAMED BY THE RENEGADE	Emily Forbes
A LITTLE CHRISTMAS MAGIC	Alison Roberts
CHRISTMAS WITH THE MAVERICK MILLIONAIRE	Scarlet Wilson

June

MIDWIFE'S CHRISTMAS PROPOSAL	Fiona McArthur
MIDWIFE'S MISTLETOE BABY	Fiona McArthur
A BABY ON HER CHRISTMAS LIST	Louisa George
A FAMILY THIS CHRISTMAS	Sue MacKay
FALLING FOR DR DECEMBER	Susanne Hampton
SNOWBOUND WITH THE SURGEON	Annie Claydon

July

HOW TO FIND A MAN IN FIVE DATES	Tina Beckett
BREAKING HER NO-DATING RULE	Amalie Berlin
IT HAPPENED ONE NIGHT SHIFT	Amy Andrews
TAMED BY HER ARMY DOC'S TOUCH	Lucy Ryder
A CHILD TO BIND THEM	Lucy Clark
THE BABY THAT CHANGED HER LIFE	Louisa Heaton

MILLS & BOON®
Large Print Medical

August

A DATE WITH HER VALENTINE DOC	Melanie Milburne
IT HAPPENED IN PARIS...	Robin Gianna
THE SHEIKH DOCTOR'S BRIDE	Meredith Webber
TEMPTATION IN PARADISE	Joanna Neil
A BABY TO HEAL THEIR HEARTS	Kate Hardy
THE SURGEON'S BABY SECRET	Amber McKenzie

September

BABY TWINS TO BIND THEM	Carol Marinelli
THE FIREFIGHTER TO HEAL HER HEART	Annie O'Neil
TORTURED BY HER TOUCH	Dianne Drake
IT HAPPENED IN VEGAS	Amy Ruttan
THE FAMILY SHE NEEDS	Sue MacKay
A FATHER FOR POPPY	Abigail Gordon

October

JUST ONE NIGHT?	Carol Marinelli
MEANT-TO-BE FAMILY	Marion Lennox
THE SOLDIER SHE COULD NEVER FORGET	Tina Beckett
THE DOCTOR'S REDEMPTION	Susan Carlisle
WANTED: PARENTS FOR A BABY!	Laura Iding
HIS PERFECT BRIDE?	Louisa Heaton